When I was a child, I spake as a child, I understood as a child, I thought as a child: but when I became a man, I put away childish things.

1 Corinthians 13:11 (KJV)

My heart leaps up when I behold
A Rainbow in the sky:
So was it when my life began;
So is it now I am a man;
So be it when I shall grow old,
Or let me die!
The Child is father of the man;
And I wish my days to be
Bound each to each by natural piety.

William Wordsworth

Part One: St. Paul's

1

Don's alarm chimed for the fourth time. The cold that should've left a month ago drafted past his underfloor heating and piled onto the reasons he didn't want to face the day. The world was against him. None of the beauty or sensual pleasure on offer — not his Moroccan master bedroom retreat nor the knockout in bed beside him — mitigated the shit show that lay ahead.

He left early after a light breakfast. Charlotte didn't eat but rose to see him off. He couldn't drop the subject of work. It was a bad habit. Always on about his project manager, an engineering puzzle to solve impossibly soon, a regulatory approval he might not get. He'd considered that the shop talk might bore her but couldn't help himself. Don hugged her, glanced at his watch over her shoulder, and strode out the door.

Work unfolded like a natural disaster. He spent the day playing catch-up, dashing between worksites, his office, and computer terminals in filthy contractor trailers. He forgot lunch and couldn't make the time to eat when he realized how hungry he was. He'd made himself too indispensable over the years. Though he'd moved into senior management, engineers were scared to sign off on permits or order materials without his approval. Don had ridden them hard, micromanaged even small projects, made them fearful.

He lied to his employees about why he needed to leave early, "I'm attending the viewing of a deceased relative." He left agitated and ordered a double scotch in the tower's concourse. His muscled body was quick for its age. It took a double to settle him. By the end of the drive home, the mental fog lifted. He tooled around his workshop, found more jobs: plans for the realignment of terraces, research into car leases – or should he keep the Maserati and do the buy-back? He ordered clothes for the wife he promised would never have to work.

"Dinner smells incredible," Don said.

"It's the coriander," Charlotte said.

"Do we grow that?"

It bothered Don that their extensive gardens didn't make them more self-sufficient. He thought that Charlotte's default solution to problems was to buy her way out of them. They'd gotten used to a rarefied palette that she plied the shelves of import food shops to support. "Dinner's almost ready," Charlotte said.

"I'll be out back." He walked to the edge of the property, a breakwater of concrete boulders, and looked down the shore at the illuminations of Lakeside Park. The town maintained the coloured lights of a long-dismantled amusement park. His first roller coaster ride was in that park with his mom and dad.

Dinner was an event. Charlotte had chosen a recipe from her magazine subscriptions. She exceeded his expectations and he forgot his claims of excess against her. Afterwards they walked down the lake road at the tempo of their conversation, rehashing the day's defeats: the political maneuvering of Don's coworkers, Charlotte's wrangling with the contractor over work delays on the sunroom, the recklessness of Sandrine's cokehead friends, and Sandrine's new puritanical streak.

"Are you happy with the addition?" Don asked. If he wanted conversation, better stick to the script. The sunroom was a diversion, a McGuffin, a prop of no value to Charlotte besides the cover it provided her. She didn't care about it and had given the contractor carte blanche choice of layout and materials.

"The window treatments look fabulous," she said. "Sand linen drapes with tassels. I'll open the box if you want to see them."

"I trust your eye," Don said.

The conversation stalled and they continued along the shaded sidewalk. The air on Main Street was lush with flowering dragon fruit and magnolia. Exotic varieties of plants and import cars provided residents with the constant assurance that the status won by moving here remained high.

"What do you think of that patterned driveway?" Charlotte asked.

"It's not stone," Don said.

"Most people can't tell genuine from fake."

Charlotte who'd grown up here and Don who hadn't were awed by the constant inflow of money to Ashfield, eternal renewal by upgrade: the installation of aggregate and tumble stone patios, screened-in porches, iron lattice balconies.

"That's a new Benz," Charlotte said.

"They've added boxwoods."

"Look how groomed and even they are." Don smiled. Charlotte squeezed his hand. They were proud of Old Ashfield.

Moving here had seemed an unattainable dream when Don was an engineering student. He was the one alumnus from his graduating class who'd become an exemplar of the field, the only one whose income could support a lakeside home here. On these walks he felt at his best. There were few moments when he felt successful: sipping scotch in the concourse of his Van der Rohe office tower; standing on the breakwater at the edge of his property, watching the pier at Lakeside Park; walking with Charlotte down Main Street in their finery. The moments were short-lived.

Don tried to make sense of this track he was on, becoming partner, updating a 1920's lakeside mansion, building a legacy of infrastructure that left no room to misinterpret the role he'd played in city building. It would be false to say he wasn't motivated by posthumous fame. Where did Charlotte fit in? She was more than proof of his success. She was the final puzzle piece that had secured his advancement. And when he made the compromises that fast-tracked his career, she'd rationalized each move. Charlotte paraphrased him, seemed to articulate what he felt better than he could. He'd stopped distinguishing between his opinions and the bugs she put in his ear. He had no other confidants and relied solely on her counsel. Yet he was starting to wonder whether her advice was in his best interest.

Charlotte knew the extent of his reliance. What she asked from him was completely different. Some of Don's clients fascinated her: media types, artists, prodigies of Toronto's creative class. She sought their approval. Rivaling them in neither education nor raw talent, she couldn't be one of them. Don was a window to their worlds. Too bad he was an introvert and withdrew from engagements.

Don stopped on the sidewalk and took Charlotte's wrist. "If I could be a silent partner, I would – if I could quit bidding for projects and keep my income."

"No one's keeping you there," Charlotte said.

"We need the money."

"Then accept your situation and move on. At least you're earning your money."

Charlotte's tone had changed lately. Don sensed her retreating from him. Despite his saggy waistline he thought Charlotte enjoyed him. What had put her off? A flaw he was unaware of, the kind that gains prominence over time until nothing can redeem it? She'd discussed having a child. Was this about kids?

"We can daytrip this weekend if you like?" Don said.

"I'd like to stay local, organize the cellar." Don knew she wouldn't be organizing anything this weekend.

"I have chores myself I should get to," Don said. "Let's go home." He felt jealous suddenly of whatever held her attention, the more because he had no idea what it could be.

Don liked having her to himself, had persuaded her that the travel in his job would make him an absentee father. "Do you want to raise a child on your own?" he'd said early on.

When Charlotte's thermostat became irregular and her fertility uncertain, she dropped the subject of children.

Charlotte stepped off the path and picked a sprig of lilac. Her unselfconscious gestures had a star quality that seduced him. He was constantly aware of her power to turn heads. With pride and longing, Don watched her drink in the flower's perfume, the olive skin of her half-shut eyelids framed by that long dark hair. He felt a new possessiveness that sharpened as she pulled away.

Over his fourteen years with Taylor Stratton there'd always been further to go: P. Eng., Project Manager, Partner. Having won all he'd set out to achieve, he felt ripped off. Work had stolen vital years. He wanted less responsibility, but the life to which Charlotte was accustomed burned through money. Mortgage payments and car leases ground on of their own propulsion. When Don proposed buying into the partnership, a colleague asked, "Who are you doing this for, Lady Macbeth?"

Don knew exactly why he'd married Charlotte. He still desired her and enjoyed people knowing she was his wife. Besides, he doubted he could do any better. How did

Charlotte feel about him? Proud? Was she playing a part?

Don stopped Charlotte on the driveway. "Maybe Brad can buy me out."

"He has that kind of money? You're growing the firm into a titan. It's too soon to walk away." Charlotte left him on the driveway and went inside.

Don had more work than he could handle. To manage the backlog, he delegated authority to young, promotion-hungry upstarts. Becoming partner required he stop engineering and trade his savings for a slight boost in salary and full exposure to the vagaries of the marketplace. Except that he hadn't stopped engineering. He'd merely supplemented his old job with the new one.

Don walked out on the breakwater. He had riparian rights, could build a dock and moor a boat here if he wanted. He remembered, after completing the final restoration job on the house, feeling nothing for the place. Charlotte appeared behind him with a tray of chocolate covered strawberries and tea.

"What a treat," Don said. He steadied himself against a boulder, made room for her next to him, but she'd already headed back to the house. A boy was skipping rocks with his dad a few houses down the shoreline. Don felt like joining in, but he'd buried his stony beach under landfill. He wound up his arm and tossed, one by one, the strawberries into the lake.

2

Sandrine was over helping Charlotte garden – keeping her company really. The tending never ceased. Weeds found a way past the screening and eco-friendly herbicides. Charlotte thought pride of ownership would compensate for the work of maintaining a house of this enormity. She hadn't appreciated the price of wealth.

Sacrifices that had seemed small and temporary at first never faded into the background the way she'd predicted. Now when her marriage came to mind, she thought of compromise and the lies she told. Her grandfather had warned his granddaughters, "If you marry for the money, you'll earn every penny," a time-tested principle revived by the marriage proposal Charlotte accepted eleven years ago.

"There's a lot more to Don than his money," Charlotte told Sandrine early on. "I trust him. He treats me like a princess. I can tell him almost anything."

"It's the 'almost' that worries me," her friend had said.

Charlotte dragged a hoe across one of the tiered gardens between the flagstone paths connecting her house to the lake. Sandrine took note of Charlotte's knowing smile. "You seem happy."

"What?" Charlotte said.

"You hate gardening. What happened?"

"Just thinking about the weekend."

"Another getaway? Must be nice."

"Don said he's going to surprise me. Sorry, I shouldn't've said anything. I know you can't get away. Your kids are so young." Sandrine multi-tasked all morning, breast-feeding and deadheading roses while they talked about their pasts and the childhood roles that stalked them into adulthood. "I don't know how you give so much to family without taking time for yourself," Charlotte said.

"I don't think about it," Sandrine said.

"At least you're not a kept woman."

"I never thought I'd feel like property until I had kids," Sandrine said. "It started when I stopped working. I'm at Sean's mercy for money and adult attention. It'd be hard to walk away — not that I want to."

"But you would walk away if you wanted to?" Charlotte said.

"Really, what am I missing? Sure, there's the lack of sleep and bickering about housework, but nothing's as important as my kids. Motherhood gives you that one certainty." Sandrine plucked Peter from her nipple and laid him in the bassinet, adjusted her bra and swiped a trail of spit-up off her shoulder, sprung the elastic from her hair and tussled out her pony tail, steps in a routine that started with dressing the kids and making breakfast, walking them to school, pushing her newborn through the grocery store aisles, and changing him in the car.

Weeding took the better part of morning. Charlotte thought it a waste of time. Sandrine talked about her kids' sports and Charlotte's mind drifted from gardening to her secret coming shift.

Some Ashfield wives were hobbyists with time and money to explore business ventures without regard to profit or threat of bankruptcy. Some had a vision and hired managers to implement it: a salon offering human-only-tested beauty products; a sportswear store with Free Yoga Sundays; a mead tasting room serving only honey-based libations.

Still other women bought existing businesses whose day-to-day operations were overseen by managers. Charlotte's job fell under none of these categories. Nor was she volunteering like many Ashfield wives. None of her friends would've guessed her employment. Don had no idea. Even on her days off, Charlotte couldn't stop thinking about work.

Charlotte collected their cups from the short grass and walked Sandrine to her van. They hugged. When Sandrine drove out of sight, Charlotte popped the trunk of her red coupe and took out a suitcase. The morning fog over the lake had burned off and the house was empty. She dumped the cups in the sink and climbed the spiral staircase to the master bedroom, laid the suitcase on the bed, and dialed the combination. She took out black nylons and a patent black leather skirt. She got a white bodice out of her dresser and found a form-fitting top in her closet. Tight fabric accentuated her curves. She tended to avoid low-cut shirts. In high school girls had remarked on the immodesty of her cleavage.

She tried this and other combos in front of the mirror, applied more makeup in a sitting than she wore around the house all week: fuchsia lipstick, foundation, thin strokes of eyeliner and mascara. If not for the stockings, she could've walked down Main Street without raising an eyebrow. She saw more daring get-ups in Ashfield bars.

Charlotte took a black clutch purse from her accessory drawer and put her driver's license, bank card, breath mints, and a thin bottle of Givenchy *eau de toilette* inside it. Her shift ran one to five, leaving time afterwards to prepare dinner and relax on the veranda before Don came home. She made sure to bring sweatpants and a t-shirt for the return trip, in case Don got home early. She'd say she was called up last minute to volunteer at the hospital.

Charlotte drove along Main Street towards the highway. Ashfield women in short-brimmed hats and oversize Italian glasses were doing what they were supposed to, buying tchotchkes, meeting friends on patios, spending obscenely. Charlotte did it all the time.

She took three highways to reach the commercial strip on Airport Road, a trip she took routinely to drop Don at the airport. Charlotte liked the tacky global Americanized flavour of pancake houses and blighted hotels. When she traveled with Don, she looked for seats in the departure lounge with a clear view to the tarmac. Planes with Celtic or Arabic scrawl on the fuselage taxied between runways and gates.

Suddenly she missed Don. He left again today like it was any other morning. The constancy of others twists the knife in a guilty conscience. Why hadn't she told Sandrine what she was up to as planned? She had to tell someone. They would've talked until dinner and this drive wouldn't be happening. Since becoming a mother, Sandrine had become very black and white. She was a family woman. Lines had been drawn. Wouldn't she perceive Charlotte as a threat?

Past the hotels bordering the airport were convention centres and discount plazas. After these, strip joints and massage parlours, lurid signs announcing 'Gold Palace' or 'Ecstasy Lounge.' Farther on, abandoned lots, auto repair shops, and more discount plazas. Farther still, transient apartment buildings rammed full of asylum seekers and recent Somali immigrants. Barren and polluted every time of day and year, a place to accelerate out of on the way to somewhere else.

Charlotte pulled into a driveway and parked behind a plaza near a loading dock. She flipped down the visor and checked herself in the mirror. Her appearance was enviable. At forty she could drink to excess, binge on fried food, pull an all-nighter, skip a shower, and come off elegant. In the humidity, without comb or hairspray, her bangs hung in tidy bundles.

She entered a windowless unit and waited in a booth-sized antechamber. A short wall separated her from a long room and hallway leading to smaller rooms. A tall black clerk of indeterminate gender, with a woman's chest on a man's frame, presided over a large binder behind the short wall. Past her was a blond woman in remarkably plain clothes sitting with a book. Charlotte thought she looked like a bank teller on break. Two women with big hair sat together in the row of seats behind Charlotte snickering, one sporting jerry curls, wide hoop earrings, and a large ass out of proportion to the rest of her. She delivered clipped phrases while the other, a skinnier version with mousy features, concealed her laughter behind her hand. They looked their parts from head to toe: stilettos, short skirts, halter tops, bleached hair, layers of foundation, rouge, lipstick, blotchy mascara. Charlotte knew the faces. She'd heard their working names when they were called to take clients — and made sure to forget them.

Charlotte greeted the clerk. "Any appointments?"

The woman checked the binder. "Three," she said. "You may also get a drop-in." Charlotte was popular. In two shifts she already had repeat customers. When the clerk called out her pseudonym, *Sherry*, she feigned surprise that a man had shown interest and sunk in her seat against the glare of the other women. If a man hesitated to choose for more than a few seconds, the clerk rang a bell summoning the rest of "the girls" from the rooms to meet the new prospect.

Charlotte had to wait an hour for her first customer. If a drop-in came by soon, she might squeeze him in before her scheduled appointment. She envied the blond woman behind her for the book she read to fill the time. Charlotte remained the picture of self-sufficiency. Really she was scared. To keep from shaking, she searched the walls for a nick or stain to anchor her attention.

Some clients' flaws were obvious: obesity, acne, a mental or physical malady. A mellow dimness clung to many of them. Charlotte tried to find something touching and irreducible in each of them. Clients came to her for more than an orgasm, which could be had more cheaply elsewhere.

More surprising was the magnetism of many clients, men who could've picked up women in nightclubs with ease, men who secretly, briefly stepped out of their everyday lives. She thought it was the smooth that exit drew them, not having to apologize for getting what they wanted and leaving when they were done. Yet weren't these life's losers, people unable to form attachments? Surely some had appealing spouses who cared about them. Why were *they* here?

Satisfaction was easy to provide, yet men sneaked out of their way to seedy, out of the way dens, funneled big bucks to pandering managers and mob-affiliated owners to get it. She never forgot that most people thought the clients were exploiters, no matter how well they paid. She enjoyed a client's defenseless gaze, took his satisfaction as a complement, carefully planned the moves that would get him off before each session.

Her first appointment on her first day was a man of no more than twenty. She had friends with sons who were older. She led him into the room, passed him a towel, asked him to take off his clothes and lie down. His wrist shook in her hand. "Have you been here before?" she asked. He hadn't. "Have you been drinking?

"Not a drop," he said. She told him the parlour rules, including one about the massage working in reverse: He could touch her. She'd left him alone to undress and went to the two-piece washroom down the hall. There were shelves containing hand cleansers and soap dispensers. A gelatinous cone of air freshener was plugged into the wall, but none of the products masked the underlying smell of the place, which was not of woman nor even of sex, but of man. She wanted to gag.

3

Father John, a tall, white-haired man in his late seventies, paused to wipe the sweat off of his forehead. A door at the side of the nave hung open, a small gesture to the muggy August heat. He sipped from a glass of water and surveyed the congregation like a lawyer estimating the general opinion of the jury, summoning strength for the closing argument. He raised his voice, "This morning, like every Sunday morning, all the runners on Main Street were getting ready for their morning runs. Do you know how many of them went to church? None, that's how many. How much of our daily activity marks us as Christians? If you were charged today of being a Christian, would there be enough evidence to convict you?" Father lingered at the altar, answered by the silence of the congregation.

Parishioners streamed onto the sidewalk after church and traded greetings: neighbours, colleagues, coaches, and their athletes. Some huddled to chat. Two young parents led their small children out of the crying room at the rear of the building. The parents, youthful at first glance, less so on closer inspection, led them towards the manicured lots of the original settlement. "I'll meet you at home soon," Sam said. He pecked Laura on the lips and hugged their children Lucy and Matthew. "Keep the car. Don't worry about me."

Sam started running. He passed the uniform shrubs and bright lawns to Main Street, where he had an appointment with his real estate agent. He stopped in front of a heritage home that had been converted into offices. A glut of sweat had seeped through his dry-fit shirt. Wearing running gear to Mass meant he could squeeze in a run before the afternoon Laura had planned got underway. His face contorted when Father mentioned the Sunday runners in his sermon. Sam had been one of them, driving half-awake down empty arterials to the Main Street Running Club on Sunday mornings for the three-hour-plus Long Run. He'd come home spent, plans for the day scuttled with his interminable recovery on the couch.

He checked one of the listings posted in the entrance, an ad for the home he and Laura had put an offer on. Then he waited in the foyer until Tony, a square-jawed agent in a sport coat, came for him. "Right on time," Tony said.

Sam followed him into a sparse office. When the Tony sat down, Sam stayed on his feet and crossed his arms. A stale smell of fast food hung in the room. "Why is our new house still listed?" Sam said.

"Not to worry." Tony got up and guided Sam into the chair opposite his. "Houses aren't removed from the listings until financing is secured. We just need a letter from the bank."

Sam's back stiffened. He leaned forward in his chair, "Our bank won't give us another mortgage until we've sold our old house."

"We made the deal on the understanding you had financing in place." Sam gripped the edge of the desk. He'd signed on with Tony because of intonation. Tony inflected the ends of statements like they were questions seeking agreement. The speech pattern gave him a vulnerable quality. Now Tony was scripted and certain, telling Sam how it was. "It's called bridge financing. Without a mortgage for the new house, your purchase is null and void."

"I've got appointments tomorrow with mortgage brokers." Sam caught the shrillness in his own voice.

Tony leaned forward in his chair. "It doesn't work like that." His eyes evaded Sam's. "It might be different if we had an offer for your home," Tony said. "As it is, there are no takers. I thought you had the money. My mistake not to request a letter from the bank."

Sam gasped, "Just give me 'til tomorrow." He took in the pictures above Tony's chair, scenes of high-performance cars and golf fairways with motivational captions — pat one-liners — each entitled *Success*, inside thin black frames.

Tony splayed his hands above his shoulders. The cuffs around his biceps stretched like stuffed sausage skeins. "We thought prices would keep climbing," he said. "For years they did. Sell a home, plow the profit into a bigger one. Banks have tightened up. Too many defaults. You're paying a mortgage for more than your house is worth — and you want a better house? What can I say?"

Sam leaned back, tried to appear relaxed. He couldn't dispel the feeling that he was overreaching — or came across that way. "So what, I lose the deal?"

"There's no deal to lose. Do you still want me to try selling your house?" Tony rephrased the question: "Do you still want to move?" The agent folded his legs. He wouldn't make money off Sam who, diminished and sunken in his chair, was a delinquent in the principal's office.

"Let me talk to Laura." Sam pried out a smile and left. He was running again, now in bursts, weaving between the throngs of Sunday browsers, past the commercial buildings on Main Street and the red brick homes near the mouth of the river, a route so familiar it haunted his dreams. He came to the end of the sidewalk where Main narrows to a single lane and moved onto the thin shoulder. He was expected at home. He wasn't going home.

Thick trees buffered wind blasts from the lake. Over two centuries the town had made a truce with nature. Ashfield was the battle-warn remnant of decades of trial and error town-building. What remained was sturdy, fitted to the landscape, an extension of it. Sam crossed the river. He remembered Tony calling this section "the affordable side of town," a tract of Canada Mortgage and Housing Corporation homes built for returning war vets. Sam stared ahead, ran faster. He had to stop at the lights for a row of turning cars. His house was off this street. He pressed the walk button twice then hammered it with his fist. Cars wouldn't shift. Sam felt out of sync with his body and the lights. Both were unresponsive. Drivers glared and honked. He felt dubious.

He moved here with Laura after they married. They'd heard about the 'rough side of Ashfield' long beforehand. Its lifeblood was Merchant Street, a main drag of Eastern European food shops and second hand stores. "Merchant Village is a community in transition," Charlotte, their realtor had said, guiding a tour from the front seat of her Continental. "Check out the funky used record store. I can see artists living above those shops." For a young couple buying what they could afford, the village wasn't a hard sell. Signs on hoarding announced, "Development Opportunity," yet no one risked building on the lots. The couple searched the storefronts for artists plying their crafts and found none. When Lucy turned three Laura said, "Our kids can't grow up here. This wasn't the plan."

Sam liked the village dives, none more so than The Shag. Mannequins in glam rock glitter suits hanged from *papier mâché* gallows in the window. Corduroy couches surrounded reconditioned spindle-legged coffee tables, salvages from Goodwill up the street. There was a sameness to Ashfield hotspots. The Shag defied categorization. Neither pool hall, bar, nor café, it was Ashfield's only bohemian hangout. Watching it recede over his shoulder, Sam couldn't fathom leaving the village, yet he'd agreed to move.

He continued past a row of ranch style bungalows. One was being replaced by a French chateau mock-up. As with most of the knock-downs, the replacement's concrete façade was textured to resemble stone and the roof pitched in the style of Second Empire mansard slate. He slowed to a weak-kneed hobble, stopped at a for sale sign. At the end of the yard, the house he and Laura had tried to buy sat empty. He walked up the driveway into the backyard, climbed the faded cedar deck, peered into the kitchen he and Laura had furnished in late-night pillow talk, crossed the grass slope to where a swimming pool might have gone.

"Yuh interested?" someone said. Sam caught sight of an oldish man next door watering hostas.

"Can't afford it," Sam said.

"You'll get there, buddy," the man said.

Sam resumed his run. He was tired of smug assurances from people he didn't think were more deserving than he was. He wondered if he lacked the credibility of other men. Or was he just unhappy? What differentiated other men from him? Sam stopped on a small bridge to tie a shoelace. The faces of colleagues and neighbours ran together in the brown finger-painted stream below.

At the town boundary, the boulevard narrowed and the sidewalk merged with the shoreline. Burlingon Bay. From here the ridge of the Niagara Escarpment is visible across the lake. Sam had reached the end of Ashfield, the natural turn-around for runners to drain water bottles and walk off soreness. He kept running.

Sam's parents drove him through Ashfield when he was ten, two hours east of their yellow brick Western Ontario farmhouse. It was one of the last towns before Toronto on their annual trip to a Jays game. His parents threatened to board him at the school that was an Old Ashfield landmark. From the window of their compact Datsun, he searched for the turret, monolithic and solid like a medieval watchtower. Running past he searched for it now, gawking as though it was a celebrity home.

Until the meeting with Tony, Old Ashfield had seemed in reach. Why had Tony led him on?

Sam's left thigh burned. His I.T. bands tightened between runs and no amount of stretching softened them. He speeded up to take the edge off. The cure for running pain was more running. His breathing settled to a conversational rhythm: the second wind, courtesy of endorphins. The sky turned otherworldly indigo.

Morning drizzle and the spume of a nearby river had thickened the air. A Doberman lay stretched out on a lawn. Sam's eyes followed the roof-lines of houses. He tried to glimpse the lives behind the recessed windows, his mind miles away, his head bowed like a penitent. He came to a subdivision, newly built on the site of an old refinery: brick and vinyl siding homes, barely distinguishable from one another by the plastic gingerbread under the soffits. A weed-strewn sign read Forest Glen or Glenforest, some English name for a wood, another development designed to look old. Could be anywhere, Sam thought. When he lived in Toronto the city had eluded him too. He'd hoped to discover some vital downtown 'scene' that never materialized. They moved to

Ashfield because Laura said it was safe. Sam was doubtful. She wanted to live on a farm. One summer in college, he'd built an addition on a St. Lawrence Valley farmhouse. The open country calmed him. Worries passed like the cumulous clouds overhead. Until he had nightmares of being swallowed by pasture and forgotten like a deserted barn.

4

When Charlotte came back in, the man-boy was lying prostrate with a towel over his mid-section. She dimmed the lights, took off her bathrobe, and rubbed the arches of his feet. She worked her way up from his Achilles to his inner thigh. He was already hard. "Turn onto your back," she said. His eyes settled on her breasts. He ran the back of his hand up her thigh and stroked her. The inexperienced man's energy and curiosity excited her. She tried to still herself, but was rocked by the beat of her own heart. Charlotte held her poise under the wave of sensation rolling along her back and thighs. She caught herself for a second, thought of Don then closed her eyes to shut him out. Her legs parted, it seemed of their own accord, and her face burned.

Logan, the parlour's operator, had warned her off of clients like him. Logan looked like any Ashfield senior manager. She guessed that he shopped in the same store where she bought Don's ties. "The temptations of the job are real," Logan had said. "The result of giving into them is always the same: submission to the client. Don't give up control." Her job was to make men climax. If a client fell asleep or ignored her, she still had a job to do, a *hand job*. If they weren't her orgasms, she reasoned, she hadn't broken vows, hadn't really cheated. Yet here she was, on the verge of climax with her first client, ignoring the implications.

The young man twitched then turned to stone. He dressed without a word and slinked out of the room. She ended the shift with two more massages, faked her pleasure through both to hasten the endings. She treated the bodies like machines in need of repair. If clients sensed her disinterest, satisfying them became impossible. Her wrists throbbed. When her job was done, she felt emptied out. Her back ached from the contorted arc she held so that clients could touch her while she worked them. She looked at herself under the cold light in the bathroom mirror. Her skin was oily and her hands soiled. The room was small and cell-like and reminded her of news footage she'd seen of Indian sex-slave pens.

When Charlotte got home, she resolved to cut ties with the parlour. At her kitchen centre island, she made salad and drained the carafe of wine she'd set aside for dinner. She left the ingredients untouched on the cutting board and slipped into reverie. That first appointment crowded out other thoughts. The impulse she'd given into at the parlour was pleasurable. It was the reality of the man that troubled her, the fact of his life outside the parlour. He'd seemed well mannered. Who was he? Why does he visit the parlour? When the questions and their hypothetical answers boiled away, what remained, distilled and pure, was a strange kind of bliss.

She thought of her own contradictions. She couldn't be herself with people and wanted it both ways, to appear prudent and be reckless. What suitor would let her be both? Anyway, she couldn't accept a partner who'd put up with that arrangement. The man she wanted, impossibly, was both her grandfather and the filthy young man at the parlour.

Then she remembered the painter who'd seduced her when she was in grade eight. He was an adult. Though she hadn't seen it that way at the time, in the eyes of the law he'd raped her. She'd told Sandrine and no one else. The secret had bound the friends. When Sandrine moved to Ashfield after she got married, Charlotte knew it was a matter of time before she'd follow her best friend there. Though she tried to forget the incident, the experience was a well to which she felt, against her better judgment, compelled to return.

5

"Such a pretty girl," the painter said. He stepped off the ladder and accepted the ginger ale Charlotte's mom had let her give him. "Thank your mom for me," he said, rubbing his thumb against her cheek. Charlotte had watched him pull into the driveway. Summer here and all her friends were at cottages. She'd stared out the window hoping a friend from her grade eight graduating class would pass by.

The painter had caught her watching him through the window and smiled. Charlotte thought he was cute. The pop was grounds to talk to him. He took a long, deep sip, suppressed a burp, wiped his forehead. "What are you up to this summer?"

"Nothing," Charlotte said.

"Are you bored?"

"Uh, yeah. I'm stuck here all July."

He pulled a pencil from behind his ear and fingered a notepad in his back pocket. "You've got me here, y'know. I'm here tomorrow too."

"Cool." Charlotte guessed he was 25.

"Can you pass that damp rag?" He cleaned a paint splotch off the walkway. "You look fit. Are you a swimmer?" he asked.

"I wish."

He walked up close to her, so his shirt brushed up against hers where it bellowed. "You've got muscular arms – not bulky though." He had square features, which his white baseball cap served to soften. "You're really toned." He stroked her outer arm.

Toned. She didn't get the meaning, but liked his touch. "You've got nice eyes, you know," he went on. Charlotte knew the boys liked her, but she wasn't used to complements. Grandma's didn't count. He stepped into the space between them. She felt a tremor in her core, but didn't recoil. He kissed her cheek then moved to her lips. She hadn't been kissed like that, with the tongue. Some of her girlfriends had, the ones who got in trouble, but not by someone so old.

He climbed the ladder. Charlotte lay down on the grass, waiting — for what, she didn't know. The air was hot. Watching him paint the side of the house with the same languid brush stroke lulled her to sleep. When she woke up he was already packed up. "Ciao, babe," he said, holding his cap aloft. Charlotte hadn't guessed at long hair when the cap was on.

She had to tell Sandrine. Her best friend was up north. Charlotte slept the night with the kiss cemented in her mind and woke up early the next morning electrified by the thought that he'd be back that day. She waited on the porch for his pickup.

"Hey babe," he hollered out the window, pulling into the driveway. He hopped down and unloaded equipment. "I'm Chris, by the way." Chris brought a radio. His style was hard rock. She liked Top 40.

"I'm thirsty," Chris said after a while. Charlotte fetched him a grape pop. "That's my babe," he said.

This time, instead of opening it right away, he set it on the ladder. "I've got an idea." He led her by the arm to where he'd stowed his equipment in the garage. Reluctant to miss out on another kiss, she didn't resist. He closed the garage and led her to the wall. "Have you done this?" he asked. The garage was musty and lit dimly by cracks in the door panels.

"Done what?"

"I'll show you." He leaned her against the cool concrete and pulled up her skirt. Charlotte was thirteen.

6

The next day at the parlour Charlotte delayed gratification until the last scheduled session, extending the high and postponing the letdown. But she'd waited too long and outlasted her client. At peak arousal she buzzed the attendant and booked one more appointment.

She was sent a man two decades her senior, obese and grubby, resembling Alfred Hitchcock. She demanded he shower first. He had an odor that came through his pores even after he'd showered and dried his skin. Charlotte winced through the procedure, as though picking soggy food from a drain. Revulsion, she learned, was an occupational hazard.

Charlotte showered then rushed home, her hair a damp mat, to make the meal she should've already started. Don usually came home after seven. The clock on her dash read 6:37. She could be home in twenty minutes if traffic was clear. Charlotte didn't know Don's car was already in the driveway. The head of Acquisitions had given him two tickets to see *Wicked* after a client bowed out.

Low late-day sun whited out the highway. Blinded drivers slowed to get their bearings. Sweat dripped off of Charlotte while the air conditioning blasted. When she was a real estate agent, before Don's firm landed the multi-year projects and paid him accordingly, she was late all the time. Buyers, anxious with their offers, became infuriated. She'd lost clients as a result. Charlotte's therapist Dr. Reynolds said she was passive-aggressive, "You test people's loyalty by inconveniencing them." Charlotte didn't agree with his diagnosis but accepted that she had a problem.

Cars bunched at the next transfer. She looked in the rearview and caught her reflection. Her eyes were her grandfather's. She remembered him always saying, "A leopard never changes its spots." She'd thought his assessments of people harsh. Now she wasn't so sure. Had she ever matured? Wasn't her work at the parlour evidence of a flaw she'd been unable to expunge from her character?

She thought of her former school run by the Sisters of Perpetual Hope, the sharp distinctions nuns drew between right and wrong. She couldn't decide what still drew her to church, faith or the warn-in comfort of habit. Father John reminded her of her grandfather. Both were products of a time, of flat-top hockey heroes and sensible Prohibition thugs, a time when people, noble or crooked, did things for reasons. That world seemed remote and fictitious. For the short while she sat in church, Father revived a view that said she was aberrant but redeemable. In secular company she felt slightly embarrassed by her faith and called it a hang up. Maybe she was overcompensating, turning to religion for a fulfillment that would be always around the bend.

Dr. Reynolds blamed her problems on her patriarchal family. But she couldn't distinguish the 'authentic self' he bandied about from the so-called 'brainwashed' part of her that resulted from upbringing. Clarity came in times of stress: the untimely death of her dad at age fifty-two, her brief cocaine addiction, the stint at the parlour.

"You believe in God out of fear," Don had said.

"I don't know why I go to church. I'm not sure that's important," Charlotte had said. Father John's sermons seemed to address her present circumstance. Was it a trick of generalization, like a cookie fortune vague enough to be universally applicable, or some freak power he had to read her? She thought of last Sunday's sermon, the Sower of Seeds. Was she the bad seed that no type of soil or quantity of water could revive?

If Don was already home, she'd say she was held up at the hospital. He didn't know she'd stopped volunteering there. She'd changed into the clothes she brought to the parlour, the sweatshirt and track pants. Don wouldn't think twice. She couldn't get used to the lying. She needed to tell someone. She might tell Sandrine, but not Father John. Hadn't she faked her confession, revealing nothing of consequence, wanting him to think her a pillar of the values he expounded in sermons?

At 7:20 Don tossed the tickets in the garbage. He combed the cupboards, found a box of saltines. When she arrived, Don said, "I was going to surprise you with theatre tickets. A bit late now." He hesitated, struck by the chance portraiture of Charlotte where she stood framed by the kitchen window. "Not to worry. How could you have known you had to be home?"

7

Teaching was never far from his thoughts. While he ran Sam planned lessons, mentally rehearsed the quips he'd tell to hypnotize students before dropping an essay on them. His department was as he imagined other ones, ranging in outlooks between crusty and zealously upbeat. Too many students cared little for the subject. English was mandatory. They needed the 'A' for the university application. Halls were lined with the pictures of teachers martyred to the cause of inspiring students who wanted a quick exit from a subject they hated.

Sam was partly bored, partly intimidated by the teachers who seemed most at ease on the job. He avoided vocation types who knew from a young age that they wanted to teach. He preferred the outliers. Some had previous careers or still harboured ambitions outside of teaching.

Maybe he could relate to them, it had occurred to him, because on the job he felt like a misfit.

In fact he was one of the better teachers, a natural who came prepared and had won the respect of the community. He still effused about books and infected students – some at least – with his passion for literature. But he felt a creeping ennui and dullness, sentiments common among the more experienced faculty. He had to dig deeper for inspiration. Had he lost interest in English? He was looking elsewhere for stimulation. The runner's high conjured moments of clarity, but he had to run farther and faster to recreate them.

It rained lightly, cooling him off. Then it came thick and fast. He took refuge under a canopy of trees.

———————

Two weeks into the job and Charlotte still felt the adolescent compulsion of her first illicit drug use. She hadn't strayed in eleven years. She thought Don had, the way his eyes followed women at functions. Between online searches for cars or vacations, she knew he surfed porn, had come in as he clicked away the images. They didn't discuss it. After late-night computer sessions, his hungry hands searched her skin. They snatched away sleep and left her churning under him.

Sandrine's husband did it too. Charlotte decided that clandestine sexual fulfillment was one of life's foul necessities. Her friend Sarah Kirby, on a surprise lunchtime home visit, had found her husband on top of a temp he met on Facebook.

Charlotte had restricted her curiosity about other men to fantasies after Don left for work. An affair wasn't an option. Like her friends, Charlotte ignored her husband's disagreeable qualities and focused on his strengths. If she and Don argued, they'd make up before bedtime. She'd ridicule the holes in the socks he refused to throw out. He'd kick over the stack of magazines she hoarded at her bedside like a messy teenager. They still laughed together and worked at pleasing each other. If she attempted a new recipe, threw a garden party that endeared him to colleagues without his having to talk to them, they were again the happy couple. Don kept up his end, surprising her with a bauble – maybe her birthstone, sapphire – bought on a trip in a last ditch scramble to the duty free shop.

In the blitz before a project deadline, Don came home bleary-eyed and voracious for drink, food, sleep, and — if he hadn't dropped off before Charlotte's bathroom cleanse — cathartic sex. She accommodated him on these days. When the project wrapped up, Don extended the weekend. They'd drive along the Rideau Canal to Ottawa or fly to Quebec and walk the old city. The compressed vacations were no break for Don, whose mind was at the office.

They'd exhausted 'couples' destinations' within a day's drive, the acclaimed Niagara wineries and boutique hotels. The daytrips had run their course. She wanted a break from him and trumped up excuses not to go, "I should clean the garage."

Don was too on top of chores. "I'll help you," he offered. To elude him, she needed to leave.

So Charlotte signed up for cooking classes. Don knew she was listless and supported her attempt at self-improvement. When the classes ended and she volunteered at the hospital, he worried where her independence might lead. Would maintaining an estate home and doing community service be enough for her? Other Ashfield wives were happy with less. If

Charlotte aspired to greater purpose, she hadn't told him. Her church attendance seemed habitual rather than spiritual. Maybe the matter of kids — not having any — meant more to her than she'd led on. Unless they experimented with fertility drugs or enrolled in the chase of adoption, that matter was settled. He'd support her returning to work, but she hadn't mentioned that either.

Before they moved into their 18-room lakefront home, it had sat empty while sweeping renovations took place. The property was weed-infested when they moved in. For months, Charlotte trimmed and uprooted while lawn care companies sprayed chemicals to thicken the grass and eliminate pests.

Feeling isolated, Charlotte invited neighbours and Sandrine to tea. The gates meant to keep people out hemmed her in, and she booked superfluous appointments with her financial planner just to get out. Women on her street volunteered at their kids' schools and organized garden parties. "Why not help Marlene with the street party?" Don asked. "There's an Ashfield Wood Association meeting this weekend."

"I'll think about it," Charlotte said. She'd already decided the Association ladies were maddening A-Types whose contributions were only surpassed by the stress they created.

She tried joining the hospital's volunteer corps. Wheeling a snack cart wasn't the in-the-trenches experience she had in mind, so she moved to palliative care — "the death ward," nurses called it. Children and women far younger than her had resigned themselves to all forms of malignancy and illness. The fumes of formaldehyde in the corridors seemed like the stench of death itself.

Charlotte waited for her third client. The bookish blond masseuse returned from one of the private rooms. Her client had scurried out the front of the building before she came back to the waiting room. That was the routine: When the customer finishes, the masseuse waits in the back until he leaves through the front door. Logan had explained to Charlotte on her first day, "A client's exit shouldn't be troubled by long goodbyes. Conversation breeds expectations."

The blond woman opened her book. Another masseuse came into the parlour and sat in Charlotte's row. After four o'clock business picked up. The flat-chested girl with mousy hair and the large-assed girl hadn't left their seats since Charlotte arrived. Clients passed them over like unsavory cuts of meat. Their nervous mirth died each time a client left with another masseuse on his arm.

When Charlotte's client arrived she didn't recognize him, though he'd requested her by name. He wore semi-casual clothes: a golf shirt, slacks, leather topsiders. If the mood was calm and she didn't feel rushed, Charlotte asked one or two nonthreatening questions: what he did for a living, where he grew up. This time she went further. "I don't think we've met. Why did you ask for me?" She stood in the doorway to the dim room, arms akimbo.

"I saw you on my way out a while back and asked who you were. I was curious," the man said.

"What made you curious?"

"You're better preserved than anyone here. Something about the way you carry yourself."

"The magic of hair and makeup, but thanks, I—"

"Can we get started?" he said. She wanted to talk about what set her apart, her big

Irish-family, growing up in North Toronto, football games on the front acre of their Gothic-revival home, the grandfather who still held a grip on her long after his death, her sense of ease when he was alive. None of it explained why she was here. The narrative she'd revised over the years about herself didn't jibe with the person in front of him. Who was she to this man, anyway? "I can't stay long," he said.

The man stepped into her path and walked ahead of her after she closed the door. Her next move was telling him to undress and lay down, that she'd be back in a minute. Then she'd undress in the staff washroom, douche lightly, dab her wrists with perfume, and return to the room in a bathrobe and felt slippers. Instead, he slipped his hand under the hip of her jeans and into her underwear. Her fight or flight mechanism kicked in, rolling her onto the balls of her feet. She pushed his chest. He grabbed her hand and twisted it. Pain shot through her forearm. Her legs collapsed so she could safely reposition her arm, but he let it go and lifted her up. His fingers found her vagina, and he gripped her against his chest with his other arm. She thought to push him away again, but he braced her under her legs and around her back like a vise. She thought to scream, but her throat choked and gurgled. She felt a second impulse, to slacken and let him take her, and her shame hurt more than the pain in her arm. A smell of red wine and lilac — something of him and of her — filled the shadowy space.

He reached his lower hand under Charlotte's backside and carried her to the massage table. He didn't force her this time, didn't ask either. He leaned her face-forward against the table, unzipped and slipped off her clothes in a uniform movement. His tongue lashed her and the tension in Charlotte's legs gave out. Her thoughts shriveled under the pulses, fear and pain yielding to pleasure. Her stomach quivered then relaxed. Having submitted completely, it was her turn. If she'd had a sharp object, she would've plunged it into him. Reciprocating his force, she worked him in her mouth as though her life depended on it. He recoiled and discharged on her. The sight of him afterwards, putting on his pants and checking the dim mirror — like he'd just used the toilet — made her vomit. Her arm ached. He stacked a layer of twenties on the massage table, patted her shoulder where she knelt, and left. She told Sandrine everything; she wouldn't tell her this. Her favourite sex was rough and by most women's standards demeaning, but this wasn't consensual or enjoyable. She should've called for help, told Logan or the police. Why she didn't had less to do with Don finding out about her job than the chance he'd learn that sometimes she enjoyed doing it.

8

"You'll think differently of me after hearing what I'm about to say," Charlotte said, knowing full well she couldn't tell Sandrine the worst of what had happened.

It was still early. Charlotte invited Sandrine over straight after Don had left for work, figuring this talk could take a while. Sandrine wasn't surprised. "You have to tell Don about the job or you have to stop. He'll find out and where will you be? It'll mean starting again. Unless that's what you want?"

"I'd rather go on as is," Charlotte said.

"That's too much work. I couldn't keep up the front if I tried. I don't have the discipline."

"Is an honest marriage even possible? I am a front," Charlotte said. "Why trouble over what can't be changed."

"I don't get you. Don't you see how fragile all this is — your lives together?"

Charlotte made Sandrine lunch. She'd expected to feel relieved by the confession, though it hadn't been complete. She couldn't tell Sandrine about that last client. Charlotte's arm ached. She should've had it seen to.

A carful of teens peeled onto Main Street. When Sam stopped at the curb to let them pass, he couldn't run. His knees smarted from the battery of footfalls and his breath had shortened. Here the lake is hidden behind thick trees and the houses are older. *The Community of Shorewood.* Farther than he thought. Too late for the afternoon Laura had planned. Once again, he'd apologize for being late and borrow time where he was already in arrears.

He crossed the street to a park along the water. Walking the shore, he thought about facing his students. If he didn't plan and mark, they skipped his class. To stay effective, he reread the novels and rewrote the lessons of courses he'd taught for twelve years. He had to suffer with students, relive epiphanies they were having for the first time, or else endure being corrected by a wunderkind on a fine point of plot. Some students enjoyed his class. At the end of term he'd find a handwritten thank you note on his desk in the English office.

A work-related problem had been troubling him. When he started at Ascension, Sam seldom left his classroom, except to visit his cubicle in the department, which was really a lunchroom. Alliances between staff had formed over time that seemed unbreakable. New teachers were regarded with suspicion, especially those who brought talent and enthusiasm. Sam kept his dealings with colleagues light. They liked his anecdotes: the gas attendant who refused to butt out his cigarette until Sam reached for the gas nozzle holding a lit match. The raccoon he found eating out of his kitchen wastebasket and allowed to come back for seconds.

Some staff gossiped about the rocky, hormonal lives of kids. Sam avoided teachers who pretended to be morally superior to their students. He hung around less conventional types who had one foot outside the school. They didn't get caught up in intrigues because, Sam guessed, they had lives outside the classroom.

He'd gotten off to a lonely start, but was buoyed a few months into the job when a teacher from Math introduced himself. Clyde was a man so successful in his prior career that he taught for amusement. He wore a jacket, not the stereotypical tweed, but hand cut linen, and a dry-fit golf shirt. Clyde was self-assured and Sam was instantly at ease with him. He could listen forever to Clyde's accounts of his days advising the Ministry of Foreign Affairs on the drafting of trade agreements, briefing the Minister about security ahead of visits to East Asia and the Middle East.

Clyde was also a semi-pro golfer. Sam muddled through a round or two a year lugging rusty clubs. He made sure golf wasn't on the menu when they got together. Clyde kept clubs and a golf shirt in the trunk of his Porsche so he could beat the five o'clock rush to the range.

Clyde was too perfect. Sam was almost relieved when he noticed Clyde's nasal tic and chronic sniffing, evidence of cocaine use. Clyde was human after all. If he could afford his habit and maintain a level of professionalism at school, Sam decided it wasn't his place to judge. Overall, Sam thought he was better for the association, that somehow it made him more real and more interesting.

When Clyde invited Sam to his house weeks into their acquaintance, Sam relished the chance to drink port and smoke *Cohibas* in the Muskoka-like backyard. Clyde was single and lived in an Old Ashfield home that Sam thought outsized for a bachelor. His foyer reeked of perfume and Sam noticed female effects in the coat closet: red raincoat, periwinkle sneakers, rainbow hemp handbag, yellow umbrella. Why hadn't Sam heard about a partner? He was curious but didn't ask questions. This was too much fun.

Twelve years on, the friendship had retained an escapist quality. They didn't talk about childhood or much personal history at all, with the exception of Clyde's previous high-flying career.

Sam was grateful that Clyde had found him a worthwhile companion and this October had invited him to his Sable Beach house. Sam didn't know if he could make the trip, being on the hook to chauffeur Lucy and Matthew to activities. He'd heard about the infamous beach house and wanted to see it for himself. Sam attributed Clyde's many invitations – to lunch, the beach house, his Lakefield Harbour sloop – to a surfeit of money and free time. There was no suggestion of homosexual advance. Though he could've been concealing his orientation, on the face of things at least Clyde was all hetero playboy, militantly so. He hadn't married and never mentioned a special someone or broken engagement. Clyde appeared impermeable to the pull most men his age feel to settle down. Sam admired Clyde's fierce independence and lived vicariously through it, knowing he could never hack Clyde's lifestyle — what he knew of it.

Sitting out on the bleachers during planning time, Sam fished for clues to Clyde's past, "Ever think about what old girlfriends are up to, how it might've been if you stuck it out together?" Sam said.

"I've never stuck around long enough to care," Clyde said.

"You must wonder what a long-term relationship is like, the compromises, seeing her at her worst, seeing her true colours."

Clyde sat up. "Why would I want to see my girlfriend at her worst?" Clyde had a taller, thicker build than Sam. His died black hair, square features, and deliberate stance cast an imposing figure. Clyde wasn't about to soften, wouldn't paint for Sam the memory of a charmed time when he fell hard for a girl, if it had ever happened, which Sam was beginning to seriously doubt.

"I couldn't be that independent," Sam said. Clyde's regime was so alien to him, yet Sam thought Clyde was more compelling than his married friends. The friendship was an alternate reality he could visit briefly and leave safely behind.

Why, then, had Clyde become a source of stress? Sam had overestimated Clyde's ability to contain his excesses. The friends covered each other's classes when one of them was late for work, but lately Clyde had been late every day. Students switched en masse out of his class before the drop deadline and administration had taken note. Clyde was a no-show at fall midterm parent- teacher interviews. Employee Relations scheduled a 'Coaching and Counseling' session, a thinly disguised disciplinary meeting.

To reel him in, Sam made oblique references to substance abuse, which Clyde didn't get or ignored. Sam had sent him mixed messages. He hadn't backed out of the trip to Clyde's Sable Beach house, which was next weekend.

As Sam stretched his legs on the shore, weighing whether to restart his run, he thought about how he could back out of the trip. Clyde would see a cooked up emergency for what it was, abandoning ship. The trip could be an opportunity to confront Clyde, an intervention.

9

Don cooked a heavy English breakfast, weekend payoff for the joyless weekday cereal and dry salad. On Sunday mornings Charlotte did step exercises and Don reclined with the paper on their 1230 square foot back deck. He looked forward to it all week. His 8:00 a.m. rise felt lethargic. In his housecoat he wielded skillets on the glass stove while Charlotte got ready for church.

Don humoured her religiosity. Allowing that religion had shaped him, he treated his Anglican background as a quirk of family history. If he joined Charlotte for Mass, it was in deference to her, out of respect.

They walked down Main Street through the original settlement to the old white church of St. Paul's. Charlotte led Don to a pew in front of a statue of Mary. Charlotte insisted they sit at the front of the transept, so she could light one of the jarred candles at Mary's feet. She perched on the kneeler in front of the flickering red jars, took a rosary out of her handbag, wedged it in her folded hands, and bowed her head. Up close, cracks in the plaster were visible through the statue's lacquer finish. The serpent under Mary's feet seemed larger than Charlotte remembered it.

Father John came into the sacristy of the old church from the side entrance. He'd made the trip from the rectory under towering blue spruces 9128 times over 22 years. He'd walk to the lake after his morning toilette and count boats, noting the heights of swells or glassy calm of the water, and look for blue herons or osprey. He'd go inside the church to find the Sunday readings and gospel, bookmark them with colour-coded ribbons, return to his paperwork in the rectory, come back inside the church to get his robe, and greet parishioners out front before the procession. If there was a Baptism, he'd remove the purpose-made earthenware jug and fill the font with water. The old priest knew sacramental procedure by rote. Sermons were harder. He tried not to reuse them, but kept them in case a crisis preempted writing a new one: the 11th hour request for Holy Unction or the drop-in confession. Office hours were ignored. A priest is always on call.

Today, a counseling spillover from the previous week: a young couple with their infant son seeking annulment. "Marriage counseling," Father told them, "is prerequisite to any discussion of breakup."

"It doesn't matter what I do," the man said. "I spell her off. I stay up to feed the baby so Mom can sleep. She doesn't appreciate me." The man was hairless and pink, a prepubescent combination of smooth skin and cracking voice. The woman unfolded her arms, blew a wisp of hair from her eyes, and began rummaging through her purse.

"Is this true?" Father John said.

The woman took out a cell phone and started texting while Father waited for her response. He didn't fill the silence to let her save face. Neither did the man. The woman grew breathy and kicked the floor before finally saying, "I make the decisions. He has nothing to say, no opinions of any kind. He feeds his face and speaks to the baby in a 'goo goo' voice all day." Her hair was coated in spray that irritated John's eyes.

"At least I take an interest in the baby," said the man. "You don't like him. I stay awake with him and *you* complain about being bored. I have to work the next day." The man's voice broke. The woman clucked her tongue each time he spoke.

Father said, "No one's responsible for making you happy. When you marry you become as one body, but you answer to God alone." When disputes were hard to unpack he liked using these words and still believed their wisdom.

John suspected that all couples arrive at the same impasse: The Immovable Other. He'd refined three decades of marital advice to one edict, which he repeated with mantra-like frequency: "A person is not a conquerable object." Father took the woman's phone out of her hand and cornered her eyes with his.

The woman, who had a habit of slouching, straightened up. "I wish he'd change," she said.

"If he changed," Father said, "you'd wish he changed again. It's easier to blame someone else."

She seemed to consider this idea. The couple stopped their attacks and promised to try again. John had nothing to add and sent them away.

Confession had taught him the universality of failure: respected parishioners in positions of authority were functionally addicted to prescription drugs, kept mistresses, skimmed company accounts. They also coached their kids' soccer and ran charity bingo on weekends. He'd reconciled himself to people's moral contradictions. His tolerance was well known. "A good priest drops self-righteousness in a hurry," he'd advised a group of newly ordained priests. "You have to believe there's hope for people. They surprise you, for better or worse, all the time."

John was still a romantic. Decades of celibacy hadn't inured him to its stricture. He subjected sensual desire to a logical gymnastics that fit it, like an errant puzzle piece, into the bigger picture of his soul's salvation. Theologically it worked, but not in practice. "From a religious perspective," John told the congregation, "attraction manifests the heart's desire for God's perfect love." Then he quoted St. Augustine: "'And my heart will find no rest until it rests in Thee.'" He believed it when he said it. Sometimes the desire for a woman's skin felt like starvation. He felt it in absentia like a phantom limb. Long ago he'd confessed his compulsion to a priest from outside the archdiocese. "For the good of the parish and the sake of your sanity," Father Michael had said, "stay in character no matter what you may feel now. It gets better. Look the part of your calling. What do you otherwise have?"

John had almost broken his vows more times than he could recall. If thought without act was sufficient to convict in God's court, he was condemned. He could've gone the other way, reached out to Anthea, the nun who led the Women's League and cleaned the rectory. She said she wanted to leave the clergy, a confession that was also an invitation. His resistance surprised him. He decided their talks couldn't continue. She was uncommitted, flighty, inexperienced. Holding his hand, she talked about loneliness. She leaned into his chest and he kissed her forehead. That was nine years ago. He'd thought her remarks about the rigidity of clerics dangerous and heretical. Tired of his counsel, her confessions stopped. She was dispatched to another Parish – providentially, he thought. Within a year she left Holy Orders.

In today's Mass he caught himself preaching to the left side of the church, watching Charlotte. Her perfect face might've been Anthea's. Their features differed sharply, but both women had the power to cut through masks. He prided himself on retaining in public the presence of mind that solitary prayer gave him. Yet these women played havoc with his asceticism. John wanted to approach Charlotte after Mass, but he was tired, and after some reflection during First Reading, too sensible to wait for her out front.

Don waited for the final blessing announcing that Mass had ended. Not until the priest had processed out behind the train of altar servers could Don coax Charlotte out of the pew. She put on her blue hat and genuflected in the aisle. The morning had started cool and dewy. It was warm by the end of Mass and Charlotte regretted her jacket. Outside she stood across from the priest, waiting for the crowd to disperse.

John had seen expressions like hers before and made a beeline to her. "Is everything alright?"

"Father, I'd like a word if you have a moment."

"Have a seat inside. I'll be right there."

Don came out as Charlotte came back in. "I need to ask the priest something for Sandrine. See you at the house." She returned to her seat by the statue. A client from her real estate days was emptying collection baskets into a large sack. *Sam*. His wife was Laura. She'd known them as newlyweds. Were they still in the house she'd found for them? Did he still teach? What kinds of lives had they made in Ashfield? His stiff walk reminded her of Don's. He'd been stylish in a creased, adolescent way, like he didn't care how down-market he looked. He was better put together now.

Charlotte had lived alone then and dated a lot. Sam had been attracted. She could tell. His eyes held hers longer than their business together warranted. He wasn't a cheater. She'd seen that too. At the time, neither was she. Men liked her. The guarded stances of their female counterparts put her on notice. Husbands propositioned; Charlotte turned them down. What might have been if just once she'd played the floozy? Don was safe. She'd taken him from no one.

Sam carried the sack to the crying room, locked it away with communion pix and collection baskets, and left by the side entrance. Father

John approached Charlotte's pew. "Nothing serious, I hope?"

"It might be," she said. He led her to the crying room. In crises, he dispensed with the Act of Contrition and penance. He believed Grace brought these souls to him. It was enough that they'd clawed their way back from darkness. It wasn't winning God's forgiveness that worried John. God's love was assured. Forgiving themselves was the challenge. These weren't the dispassionate regulars who treated confession like a hair appointment. A penitent's humility humbled him. He tried only to listen. What needed saying would come.

"Don and I are at an impasse. I've thought about other men," Charlotte said.

Father John asked questions which she answered, but he detected omissions. Her confession was incomplete. Her remorse seemed extreme in relation to the sin. She'd left out the parlour, saying only that her thoughts had strayed from Don. He waited for details that never came, signed the cross on her forehead. "Talk to Don if your attention drifts," he said. "Revive what first drew you to him – and don't lie."

She picked up a worship hymnal in the pew, flipped the translucent pages. "If anything changes, Father, I'll let you know." After she left, Father stayed there in the semi-contemplative state that was his comfort zone. He took a brooch out of his sash: gilded silver filigree with a fake ruby at its centre, the kind worn to 1930's dance halls. Aside from some black and white photos, it was the only keepsake from his mother's estate. John's dad had died before he could remember. In the military portrait on John's nightstand, his dad looked much younger than his son. It made John forever imagine Dad as that youthful corporal fighting for the Brits, returning to his wife and small boy after the war, chasing work in dirt poor Ireland.

The brooch looked like the toys in the crying room. It fit in with the plastic Barbie cameo and *What Would Jesus Do?* rubber bracelets. John's mother had worn it on her lapel. The picture stuck of his sepia mother in brown wool jacket, cotton skirt, and pillbox hat: the sole provider, barely twenty, fragile and overwhelmed. When consumption had taken his dad, she didn't blink, got on with the business of raising kids. John felt he understood Charlotte. Her successes, like his, had come too easily. She hadn't come up hard like his mom. No real problems so she creates some. He thought it was a theme with their generations.

Don could tell she wasn't right. Charlotte stayed downstairs baking and watching silver screen classics – James Cagney in *Yankee Doodle Dandy*, Natalie Wood and Warren Beatty in *Splendor in the Grass* – until he fell asleep. Breakfast was waiting when he got up. Charlotte stacked plates, checked voicemail, made lists. If she got up early, she trifled in the garden. She was turning away from him, but Don daren't draw attention to the fact, in case his worst suspicions were born out. For weeks now she hadn't taken calls in the afternoons. Her cell was left switched off. Charlotte was quick with answers, "I was in a mall where there's no service." "I forgot the charger. The battery died." "I forgot to bring it with me." He didn't pursue it, didn't want to seem possessive.

Then there was the night he'd gotten the theatre tickets. She'd come in breathless with wet hair, muttered something about showering at the hospital. He didn't believe her.

Don sat for a while on his deck. There was a chill off the lake. He ran upstairs for a sweatshirt. In the corner of the walk-in closet, beneath the shelves where his sweaters were stacked, he found a gym bag. Charlotte didn't exercise much and he was curious. Feeling around inside, he was surprised by the softness. Not the rough gauge of a track suit. When he emptied the bag, he found the lingerie he'd bought Charlotte to prod her into seducing him. She'd worn it too, early in their marriage. Why was it in the bag?

He brought the bag to the kitchen and dangled it over the counter where Charlotte was washing pans. "I was giving them away," she said. "You know I don't wear them."

"I'd hoped you would."

Charlotte dried her hands. "Sure, why not?" She took the bag upstairs. Her hands were wet though she'd dried them and her face was pale. What was she thinking leaving out that underwear? Sandrine was right. There was no end to the lies she'd have to tell.

She considered telling Don, but decided that relieving her conscience wasn't worth hurting him. Guilt spoiled simple pleasures: food, her wine aperitif, evening walks with Don. She had to get off topic. Staring out the window above the sink at the fussy terraces, she felt like a squatter in her own home. It was someone else's.

10

Ashfield is quiet in late summer. Main Street residents who've made their fortunes make summer last in northern cottages. By the end of September, the river valleys of Bronte and Sixteen Mile Creek channel cool northern currents to the lake. Shadows lengthen; sweaters come out of storage; winter begins its steady march.

Sam returned late from his long run to Laura's silence. He'd apologize like all the other times. Sam knew it wasn't fair. She got less time to herself than he did and would be climbing the walls when he got home. Lucy and Matthew would demand he take them to the park or read them stories.

"Where in hell were you?"

"Sorry," Sam said, "I sorta got lost." Laura shook her head, returned to chores in the kitchen.

"I'll make it up to you," he said.

"You'll give me a four-hour break?"

Sam's concession was to pack his family in the car and drive north to Rattlesnake Point, a patch of nature in the asphalt sea between Niagara and Toronto.

They hiked and watched turkey vultures dive from sandstone cliffs. Sam carried Matthew in a backpack. Lucy ran alongside to keep up. Sam's legs burned from the run and he tripped over dead branches. They stopped at the edge of a canyon and looked for animal shapes in the clouds. When Sam moaned about his legs, Lucy mocked him through fractured nursery rhymes:

Hickory Dickory Dock
The dad hiked up the rock
Tripped on a branch and tore his pants
Hickory Dickory Dock

Sam chased the kids around a giant boulder and tickled them to hysterics. On the drive home, cresting the escarpment face onto a steep road, a necklace of city lights rose below. Laura leaned forward. "Beautiful," she said. The day was salvaged. Sam pushed out thoughts of the coming beach house weekend. He had to be present.

She'd taken the news of his meeting with Tony well. "I can wait to move," Laura said. "We don't need to live in Old Ashfield." She was shorter than him. When she mashed her head into his chest he folded her in his arms. She got on with dinner preparations as though the home was an ill-conceived dream best forgotten. He knew she wouldn't forget.

After dinner they sat on the porch. Laura and Matthew tiptoed behind a robin needling the grass. The lopsided screen door Sam installed without a spirit level slammed. This unglamorous life, it turned out, was the one Sam wanted. He stared at the lines around Laura's brown eyes and thought, *She's still beautiful*. They drifted in and out of sleep, holding hands. Lucy and Matthew played in a cave of cardboard boxes.

Laura sorted the mail that she'd tossed by the door Friday night. Sam pulled a newsletter out of the pile. Their address was handwritten on a white label. Beneath the headline "Homes Recently Sold In Your Area" were pictures of houses, bungalows like theirs. A gold *"Sold"* ribbon tied off each photo at the top right corner, below that a picture of his former real estate agent, Charlotte. Her hair was feathered 80's with soft luminous background, the kind used in glam shots of aging actors.

Sandrine and Charlotte carried the files out of the attic and filled the trunk of the coupe. Sandrine had dropped her kids at daycare so she could help Charlotte set up her cubicle in the realty downtown. Some of her colleagues from eleven years ago were still there. A woman who started just before Charlotte quit leaned over the receptionist's desk. "Everything alright? I thought you were done with real estate." Charlotte knew the face behind the flaking foundation, but couldn't place the name.

"Things are fine. I miss work is all. Our home's how we want it. Not much to do there. Don's cut back his hours. I figure, my turn to pick up the slack." Charlotte said what she thought was expected of her. The office stirred memories of the petty feuds and laughs, the razor sharp bite of them, also the camaraderie of toiling together. Colleagues had respected her — to a point. When sales thinned, if her dry spell persisted while others sold, the rumblings started: conversations died in her presence; politeness replaced easy banter. Lucky her slumps didn't last. She knew whom not to trust.

Can I be trusted? Charlotte thought. If she cared about Don, why had she deceived him?

She remembered Father John's advice: "Revive what first drew you to him and don't lie." She'd thought it quaint at the time. He'd tried to help her. What advice could she expect without telling him what she'd really been up to?

Charlotte emptied a box of old stationary and stared into space. She wasn't crying, exactly. When Sandrine came in with another box from the car, Charlotte was bent over files rubbing her eyes. Sandrine pulled her out of her chair like a toddler from a snow bank. "Get your mind off yourself and back on your job."

In a solemn voice Charlotte told Sandrine about the rape.

"Why didn't you call out when he grabbed your arm?" Sandrine asked.

"I froze."

"Why did you satisfy him after he hurt you."

"I don't know. Once I thought I couldn't overpower him, I made the best of things."

"You could enjoy that?"

"I thought I couldn't leave."

"We shouldn't talk about this here," Sandrine said, but they were too far gone.

"There are boundaries, Charlotte. I can't make decisions for you, but I'll tell you what I think. You have more to offer than seduction. There are worthier causes than the sex-crazed and attention-starved. What were you thinking? People are ruined by a lot less. Did you go to the police?"

"No."

"Do you plan to?"

"No." Charlotte sneezed into a clump of tissue.

"I don't understand you," Sandrine said. She went to the car to get more boxes.

Charlotte searched old realty files for former clients. Tracking one down would give her an in. She was taping photos from a trip down south with Don onto her cubicle when the woman she met in reception came by. "A lot's changed," the woman said. "Andrew and Sheila retired. Vernon left the brokerage. Paul's still here — and me. I'll have to introduce you to Tony. If you need anything at all, let me know." Charlotte wanted to take the woman at her word, to find her helpful. On the way to her corner office, the woman's heels echoed down the hall. Janet's her name, Charlotte remembered.

Sandrine unloaded the last box of files on the beige desktop. "I've gotta pick up my kids," she said.

Charlotte organized contacts by location, relying at first on the brokerage's brand to lure clients. She searched the rolls of homes sold and put together distinct newsletters for each community: Brookfield, East Ashfield, Uptown Ashfield, Morrison, Old Ashfield, Westfield Trails. The communities of longest-standing were easy sells, none more so than her backyard of Old Ashfield. They were also hardest to break into for a new agent. Charlotte had her good reputation to add to the testimonials of past clients. One commission in her exclusive enclave was an enviable year's salary.

"I'm not about the money," Charlotte told Janet. "I'll help clients find the best homes they can afford." Janet guffawed and sat down next to Charlotte.

"I'll support my sellers too," Charlotte said. "I won't undersell for a fast commission. If a client can hold out for a higher price, so can I."

"How nice for you," Janet said, deadpan. "Wish I could wait for the perfect sale. I need a steady income. You'll have to make quota yourself, you know. Office space isn't free." This younger woman who'd stayed on at the brokerage after Charlotte left, it turned out, was her boss. Her visit wasn't a social call and Charlotte's sales philosophy had made Janet cringe.

"Selling in this market will be tough," Janet said. She was right. Home prices were in free fall. Who had the money or guts to ride out a decline with no bottom in sight? Charlotte still liked real estate's long term prospects. People need to live somewhere. Those forced to sell stood to lose the most: overburdened debtors, newly minted unemployed, company transfers. The bank manager posted to Calgary branch effective next month.

Charlotte had started her real estate career in hard times and learned on the job. She'd resigned battle-hardened and effective, the way Don found her when he became her final client. "I knew you were the right agent," he'd said. "because I'd buy anything you sold."

"I began as an imposter," she'd told him. "I didn't get negotiation, how to sweeten a deal without giving away the farm. Clients must believe they're getting the best deal."

This time there was no question of Charlotte's ability. Secure in her finances, she took the brokerage's least profitable clients: rentals and first-time home buyers trying to gain a toehold in the market. At Charlotte's first performance review, Janet warned, "This isn't a nonprofit, you know. We're not in public housing. There are easier ways to make money."

"Moving people between palaces doesn't cut it for me anymore."

"I don't get you," Janet said. "It's a job, not a cause. Yet you're closing deals in a tight market. You've taken needy, low commission clients that no one else wants. I'd throw you a cherry, an estate home or commercial plaza, but I know wouldn't care."

Sam and Laura read their bills, a departure from stuffing them in a folio and pretending they didn't exist. The debts had gotten away from them last summer. They'd registered Lucy in dance with what remained of their savings. The credit card bill with the Disney trip on it arrived then they couldn't pay their mortgage. It took a year to silence the collection agencies.

They'd become acquisitive again. Tony had shown them houses in Old Ashfield all summer, had sniffed out their financial disarray, dug up their nets worth. They said they could handle a larger mortgage. Tony played along. Weren't credit unions flogging no-money-down, 40-year mortgages you could carry to the grave? He'd seen a lot of it lately, clients living beyond their means, skipping the steps his parents and grandparents took to get ahead.

On every street homeowners teetered on the edge of default. Nationwide, families had bought into the myth of endless growth. The housing crash exposed the lie.

Tony left the matter of financing to the end, preserving for Sam and Laura the illusion that they could afford their lakeside dream.

———

Sam lay down beside Lucy and Matthew and harangued them: "Is your homework done? Were you included in baseball today? Don't let Chloe push you around." He kept tabs, feared becoming an absentee father. Matthew climbed into his lap. Lucy nuzzled his side. They could sleep now.

Sam slinked out of the house and walked to The Shag. He took a stool by the window, watched patrons of the coin laundrette across the street, a plain brick and Masonite building with a glass storefront. A woman and man stood apart folding clothes into piles. Sam guessed they were college students. He wondered if the man, who kept stealing glances at the woman, would make an advance. Increasingly Sam's outings consisted of vicarious observation. Others took risks while he watched from a safe distance.

A woman in a raincoat whose face he didn't process right away breezed past on the sidewalk. An old girlfriend? A friend of a friend he met once and hoped to meet again? The realtor on the bulletin: *Charlotte*. He'd almost called to ask that she take over his home search from Tony. At first he watched her from safety like he'd watched the customers of the launderette. Then he ran out after her. She was halfway down the block. "Charlotte Granville?" He caught his breath. "Not sure you remember, Sam Hennessy? Hope I didn't scare you. You found my first home."

"I remember. How've you been?" Charlotte said. She looked him over. It all came back.

Sam rolled back on his heels. "This is my local. Join me for a drink? Course I'll buy." He remembered her peeking at him over the purchase agreement for his first home. A second of eye contact had said how she felt. The attraction was reflexive and she wouldn't have chosen it. He felt like he was on top of a mountain he'd spent his life climbing and suddenly saw his true destination on another peak, too far gone to start over. He'd been decisive in his commitment to Laura.

"Why not? I have no appointments in the morning," Charlotte said.

They walked back to The Shag. He was nervous. The candles had been extinguished. There were no other customers. "It's eleven years since we bought 219 Wesley. I don't see your ads for a decade. Your newsletter arrives last weekend and here you are."

"I don't officially exist," Charlotte said. "I'm in witness protection. I married a mob boss." She laughed.

"I believe you," Sam said. He ducked, pulled his coat over his head. "Has anyone seen us together? I was never here."

Charlotte howled. Sam was relieved to see her being playful. He remembered her as being the bottled up sort. The mob metaphor was apt. He could see her in hiding, surfacing incognito to buy groceries. He thought of his own secret identity, the furtive ways he expressed it.

Sam stared while Charlotte took off her coat. She might as well have stripped. When she gave him her full attention, his confidence tanked. What could he say that would be of interest to her?

"I just got back into real estate after a long, messy hiatus," Charlotte said.

"Last we talked you were getting married."

"I might be getting a divorce." The weakness of their affiliation made it easy to be honest. She still found Sam attractive; she also doubted that he'd cheat. He wore the family badge too well. She liked it on him, would let him vent about his marriage if it helped him. In exchange she might say something surprising about herself. The Shag's owner Cal cleaned their table.

"Divorce?" Sam said.

"If I'm not careful."

"So you're testing boundaries?"

"No, I crossed them. I'm still crossing them."

"I don't follow. Do you want to stay with him?"

Charlotte waited until Cal had gone. "In theory," she said.

"So you need to make a choice."

"I know what I should do."

"What could be so bad?"

"What do you think I'd do with free time?"

Sam suggested pastimes he associated with her status: spinning class, sculpture, community theatre. Charlotte told him about the parlour. He'd visited places like it in college, a pricey diversion for a man making the most of an education he could ill afford. He'd felt a bit pathetic going, but decided that he wasn't above being pathetic.

Faking high-minded concern, Sam listened longingly to every detail of her account, imagining himself on a table under her arms, tugging the cuff of her underwear as she reached over him.

"I understand if you're disappointed," Charlotte said. "Talking helps. I need to be myself around somebody."

"I get it. You usually do what people expect. You need an outlet for what remains."

"What I want is always elsewhere."

"You seem to have a lot. Sounds like we could both be more appreciative. What's that Martha and the Vandellas line, 'nowhere to run, nowhere to hide'? But you shouldn't feel trapped. I don't," he lied. "I'm here with you." Sam waited for Charlotte's response. When it didn't come he filled the dead air, "We follow the scripts for the roles in which we're cast."

"I think people can change," Charlotte said. Sam doubted that she believed this.

Charlotte stared into her glass. Sam said, "What you did is no worse than what men do all the time when they think about other women – like I did just now." Dealt another pause, he looked out the window at the people leaving bars after last call. "Betraying Don is wrong," Sam said, "but we all betray. You decide how much betrayal you can live with." The conversation had gotten heavier than either of them wanted.

Sam asked Charlotte about her job, the challenge of matching buyer to home, success resting on the trust she instilled. "To earn clients' trust," Charlotte said, "you have to trust yourself."

He figured she was embarrassed by her account of the parlour and tried to put her at ease by exposing his own foibles — the debts, the failed home purchase, his escapism through Clyde, the half-baked plan to reign him in this weekend. "What are you after, home status? I can find a lender who'll approve a mortgage."

He considered her offer. "I've already consolidated debt and hustled more credit. It's too much work." His shirt caught on the splintered arm of his chair. He was suddenly aware of his clothes, cheap and dated compared to Charlotte's crisp new outfit. Outside it began to snow, a light April dusting. The bar felt warmer. In silence they watched flakes glide and melt on the asphalt.

"It's not status I'm after," Sam said, "it's probably freedom."

"Freedom to be what? A rootless wreck like Clyde?"

"He doesn't fascinate you a little?"

Charlotte reminded Sam of stand-out women etched in memory whom he dated and imagines are now happier and more successful than he is.

Sam showed her the 70's kitsch on the walls: celebrity magazine covers, discontinued stubby beer bottle labels, the jerseys of bankrupted hockey franchises. "I feel at home here in the village," Sam said. "If we move house I won't be coming here anymore."

He talked about the settlers who built Merchant Street: Polish, Ukrainian, and Irish diggers of water mains and the first brick homes west of Toronto. "They grew vegetables in allotments near the tracks to carry them when the work thinned out. Banks refused them loans, called them gypsies."

Charlotte perked up. "You romanticize a golden age of honest labour that never existed. People worked hard then because they had no choice."

"Prosperity has come too easily to our generation. It's made us indifferent," Sam said.

"Life's better today. Appreciate what you have."

"Maybe it's not generational. Maybe it's a feature of places like Merchant Street. People here have earned what they have."

"You don't know who's earned what or how grateful people are. The have-nots are *not* happier."

"Okay, I'll speak for myself. I'm a malcontent. Wish I knew why."

On this point she relented. They'd washed up on the common ground of their discontent. *Misery loves company.* Sam was grateful to let down his guard. Cal and his girlfriend stacked chairs for closing.

Sam walked her to the end of her driveway. "You can come in if you like," she said, hugging him. He felt her warmth come into his skin. He wanted to follow her in. Her jacket pulled away from her neck like an offering. He kissed her skin and she looked at his face to draw meaning. He backed away, folded his arms, said goodnight, and left.

11

On the beach road, they stopped at a fill station. Clyde got out of the car to fuel up. Was it boredom, curiosity, the chance to catch Clyde out that spurred him to search through the glove compartment? Clyde's CD's were alphabetized and shelved neatly in the Porshe's centre console. Perhaps Clyde stowed his coke in the same fastidious manner, in a cigarillo box fitted to the compartment. Sam's suitcase contained the remains of past vacations: crumpled boarding passes, lollipop wrappers, miscellaneous adapters for defunct hand-held devices compressed into the bottoms of side compartments. The refuse of family life followed Sam everywhere. For sanity, he'd given up hiding it, whereas Clyde purged non-essential clutter without delay. His workspace, his car, his great room coffee table, were clinically spare.

So Sam was shocked to find the glove box stuffed with frayed business cards. They read like the caption headings of garden variety sex-for-hire ads, the kind dispensed in casinos and left on windshields in motel parking lots: *24/7 Cat House, Bitches in Heat, BBW Afro Massage, Greek Fantasies Fulfilled.* Without reading it, he slid one of the cards in his breast pocket and shut the compartment.

The April Saturday morning was summer-like. On the basis of the pictures he'd seen of beach frontage and expansive rattan furniture, the setting promised to be memorable. Laura had given him a rare free pass, thinking an occasional "boys' weekend" might stave off a mid-life crisis.

The beach house exceeded expectations. The kitchen walkout faced a grove of tall white pines bordered by flagstone paths and reflection pools. The interior was the picture of post and beam purism: Scotch pine plank floorboards, hand-crafted driftwood tables, maritime blue-grey trim around windows and doors. Sam noticed evidence of female activity in the coat racks and bathroom cabinets: a straw bell hat, purple windbreaker, Lululemon hoodie. When Clyde left the room, Sam searched the drawers, cabinets, and sconces for more signs.

The afternoon was uneventful and Sam felt silly about his doubts. They sunned on deck chairs on the wet sand and sipped martinis.

Clyde said, "There's an oyster bar in town I want to show you. It's full of townie cougars. A bit rough but there's a band and the place does a mean grouper sandwich."

"I'm in," Sam said, his appetite fueled by the long morning drive and afternoon sun. At the rooftop tiki bar, Sam was uncharacteristically loose-tongued. He didn't drink much these days, and Clyde seemed receptive to Sam's soused blather. "So glad I came. I don't know how you do it though Clyde, any of it, staying single, the beach house."

"I'm glad you could make it. To more nights like this!" Clyde said. Glasses clinked.

"But I gotta say, buddy, it's a lot of plates to keep in the air," Sam said.

"I don't follow."

"Y'know, the blow, the ladies."

"What do you know about '*blow*'?"

"C'mon, I see you after washroom breaks at school. You come back practically levitating."

"Let me show you something," Clyde said. He led Sam out of the restaurant, his gait wonky from all the drink. They reached the parking lot and Clyde's Porsche. Clyde pressed the trunk opener on the remote. "Check this out." Sam looked in the trunk at a row of clear plastic bags full of grey power.

"What's that, coke?"

"Heroin."

"You're fucked."

"This is nothing. You should see what I've got at home. Don't ask." He chuckled, "You need plausible deniability if you're questioned. Relax, I'm kidding."

"What are you into?" Sam said. His breaths had shortened. He felt sweat gather on his forehead.

"You don't want to know."

"And what's this about?" Sam said. He pulled the business card he'd stowed earlier out of his shirt pocket.

Clyde let out a loud, florid laugh and leaned into Sam, "Dude, you have no fucking idea. I'll take straight you to Sodom and Gomorrah. There's a special place in hell for me."

12

Father returned to the rectory for a sherry. Marriage counseling had finished him. In every case he could tell one of the spouses wanted out but acted as though the problem was more complex and profound than distaste. He understood the meaning of denial.

Father John Arthur Shaunessy had come to the Jesuits from a position of weakness. He'd been a heavy gambler in Ireland, a "Prodigal" as he told it, who'd squandered sales income and extorted pension from his mom to feed his addiction. Baccarat and horse racing took his car then his flat then his job. He'd used sick days to play the high-roller tables of private clubs, always with the plan to stop after one last big haul which never came. Approaching thirty, the age by which his cousins had established careers and families, John was on a tear. When the court set the terms of repayment on his 38,000 punt debt, he turned up in the confessional of St. Stephen's Parish. His mom had stopped taking his calls.

The Pastor saw potential in John, a devil may care charm that, with guidance, could lighten burdens. He gave John grounds work and let him live rent-free in the visitors' suite until the creditors backed off. John called this time his 'Road to Damascus.' He told his story as a message of hope when he found someone distressed and alone in a pew. "Is anything troubling you my child?" he'd ask in his Irish lilt like in the movies. But the plights that parishioners poured out to him followed a pattern that John spotted too soon. They were caricatures who'd made foolish choices and should know better. He'd become callous.

John figured Don was another marital discard. Charlotte said she wished Don worked less. John didn't believe her. Wasn't she projecting, making her indiscretion out to be John's? He still didn't know what the indiscretion was, didn't need to.

Running the parish had become a bother. For years he'd told the flock God was all they had. It seemed truer to him now than ever. He'd retire soon and live out his days as an attendant priest, handing over paperwork — Baptismal certificates, Pastoral letters, the issuing of charitable tax receipts — to a young priest bent on theological correctness as he'd been not long ago. More time to tease kids in the crying room and listen to Charlie Parker recordings in his bedroom.

Through thirty-one years he'd tried to be a worthy servant. When good intentions failed he still had the sacrament of Reconciliation and the Catechism. Retirement wouldn't be so different from his work life, and couldn't come fast enough.

_____

Sam had never run this far from home. He rested on a damp wooden bench by the shore, gulped water from a bottle he toted in an elastic belt, and vomited most of it onto the sand, the taste of last night's Tequila still in his throat. He dropped his socks and shoes near a small hillock where the water laps the shore, and walked on the beach watching the steel works blaze across the bay.

Where he'd found the energy after last night's binge and today's drive from Sable Beach was a mystery to Sam. He ran as far as his legs would take him, with no view to getting back. He'd run forever if he could, long enough that the night with Clyde vanished in the soreness of his legs. Then he wouldn't have to think about distancing himself from Clyde at work.

Clyde's past was a fabrication: the international trade consultant, the semi-pro golfer, the ladies man. He was a top to bottom fraud, a common dealer and miscreant philanderer. The school board was building a case for his dismissal. Dots would connect through some misstep: a false insurance claim or slur of speech at a police check. Clyde's movements would be tracked, the backgrounds of contacts checked. Then would begin the issuing of warrants and the laying of charges. Sam's name couldn't be attached to any of it. If Clyde had been honest from the start Sam might be more understanding, but then they wouldn't have grown this close.

Sam was on the road again, sand from the beach shredding the skin between his toes. He passed the last of the houses before the commercial strip of Merchant Village. The sun dropped out of view. Clouds fluffed and tailed off like bails of smoke, blue sky reemerging from behind white palls.

On Merchant Street a line was growing outside Ashfield's soup kitchen. A Salvation Army coffee truck parked beside the crisis centre next door. The patrons lined up were all men, most of them wearing dark jackets, the mud-navy colour of security guard uniforms.

Sam stopped running. His legs seized up. Unshaven and light-headed, he limped past the line on the boulevard. But for the shiny running clothes, he looked like any one of the men lined-up. He breathed unsteadily. *Almost home.*

A familiar figure sat next to a thin, purple-nosed old man who sniffled and coughed. *Charlotte.* She was holding the man's hands, an artless gesture that was intended to help. Her eyes never left the man she was consoling. If they did, she would've seen Sam, who felt unearthly, unrecognizable, all spirit.

———————

Sam's smart phone rang again as he entered the English Department. He switched it off, feeling toxic every time he saw Clyde's name on the screen. Sam had ignored the texts asking him to cover Clyde's class, deciding to let him sink this time.

Students waited outside the class for Clyde. Twelve minutes after the bell, Clyde ran down the hall in the crimped sweatshirt and shorts he'd worn on the drive from Sable Beach, rank with alcohol and body odour. He pushed open the unlocked door, chastened the class for not having the sense to go in before he arrived.

Vice-Principal Joe Chen had been watching from the end of the hall. Clyde read the homework board to figure out where he'd left off in the lesson. When he turned around, Joe was at the door with a rookie supply teacher who took charge of the class without introduction. Joe escorted Clyde to the office. The police who'd followed Clyde to work were waiting in the foyer to impound his car and lay charges. They put Clyde in the cruiser. Sam watched from the English office window while colleagues gave a play by play between hoots and jeers. Clyde was suspended with pay pending investigation.

All week Sam redirected questions from students who'd seen them together often. He avoided the English Department, where an inquisition about the weekend lay in wait.

Sam hadn't realized how favourable his association with Clyde had been to Clyde. It was because Sam hadn't covered for him that day that the office had acted, and Sam knew it.

The following Saturday he received a string of texts from Clyde. Instead of reading them Sam stowed his phone in his dresser and changed into running clothes. He ran down an old hydro corridor which led to a river trail, stopped at a lookout on top of a gorge. Runners and hikers break for water and gels on the small perch. A mom who'd slinked out to jog while her baby was asleep was leaning against the railing.

Sam normally kept his greetings conventional. Instead he said, "You look fabulous."

"Keep talking," the woman said and laughed. "I gave birth eight weeks ago. I'm trying to get my body back."

"I'm sick of training and don't know how to stop," Sam said.

"You're an addict."

"Maybe." Sam got back on the trail, called out, "And you do look fabulous!"

He passed a pack of runners from his old club. One of them hi-fived him. Another called, "Join us." Sam considered it, but they were on a set path. He preferred unplanned routes.

His clothes were damp when he got home. Laura came onto the back deck with a glass of water. She'd heard him coughing on the way in.

"I like it here," Sam said. "I'm not ready to move."

"You can leave a place too soon," Laura said.

"Things could've gone differently. Look at Clyde."

"You're nothing like him."

"Thanks, but I know that's not true."

He kissed Laura's nose and went to their bedroom, took the cell out of his drawer and read the texts he'd ignored, abbreviated pleas from Clyde: "2/2 me please," "r u there?" Sam scrolled down his contact list to Clyde's name, punched the green button.

Clyde answered after one ring. "I knew you'd call," he said.

"Before you breathe another word," Sam said, "understand that I knew you as someone else. I can't answer Clyde because I don't know him. I can't know him. People depend on me."

"I get why you're walking away. It's enough to know that you care how I'm doing."

"What will you do?"

"They haven't fired me. I'm under investigation for trafficking. The evidence is all circumstantial."

"I haven't been questioned. Keep me out of the loop."

"They've got nothing," Clyde said.

———————

"I can't come back to the parlour," Charlotte said.

"I didn't expect you to. It's been over a month," Logan said.

"I'm sorry." Charlotte wiped down the faucet with her free arm. She had no plans but to dust and glory in the house's perfection. She felt unequal to the task.

"I don't know what brought you here. You don't need the money," Logan said.

"I don't know either. There's a part of me I can't share with Don – with anyone, I've started to think."

"You're not a bad person," Logan said.

"I'm a bad wife."

"You won't have to lie anymore."

Charlotte tossed the rag into the sink. "I doubt I'll stop lying."

"I hope you find happiness, Charlotte. Our girls want the life you have."

———————

Charlotte lit a candle and took her customary seat by the statue of Mary. In another pew Sam and Laura shared a missal and followed along with the scripture reading. Matthew absently answered each prompt to sit, stand, or kneel. Lucy ran swatches of hair between her fingers. She hadn't heard a word and stared at the clerestory, daydreaming. She was Sam at her age.

Having read the Good Samaritan parable in Luke, Father John delivered the homily. "You choose your friends, not your family. Jesus asks us to go further. He says we shouldn't even choose our friends, but open our hearts to everyone." Charlotte looked for Don's arm in the empty seat beside her. "How often do we see the suffering right in front of us? Unless it's easily recognizable – the blind man with a cane, the infirm man in a wheelchair – we don't bother. We donate, throw money at problems, shut our eyes to the poor in spirit." Matthew was checking out girls in nearby pews, and a few much older women. Charlotte was one of them. "Sometimes helping means paying attention. Do we make the time? 'He will answer them, I assure you: Whatever you did not do for the least of these, you did not do for Me either.'" Father John left the altar to sit on a wide-backed chair at the side of the chancel, giving his flock time to ruminate before the Nicene Creed.

Charlotte and Don's conversations sank to a colourless exchange of facts. Gone were the elaborate meal preparations and after dinner walks. Don stayed in the city to avoid the new dinner arrangement: heating up single-serving frozen dinners and eating them alone in the atrium.

One morning while he shaved and Charlotte sorted laundry on the bed, Don said, "You didn't bother with me when you were at home all day. Now that you're working, you don't want to be here at night. Why not move on?"

Don might've mentioned a leaky pipe, Charlotte thought. He wouldn't defend their marriage. In fact, neither would she. Charlotte put on a vest and scarf and walked through the gardens she'd realigned, working out the impact of a split. The house would be sold, the assets divided. "I'll do the paperwork," Charlotte offered Don. "The place'll go fast."

It surprised her how adaptable to single life she could be after eleven years. She was in her old job at the brokerage, looking for a lakeside apartment like the one she had before Don, as though marriage had been a temporary leave from the person she'd always been.

Sam searched the stained glass figures of saints and the eyes of parishioners. The faces he saw were all Clyde's. He spotted Charlotte in the front pew, head bowed, eyes closed. He watched Lucy twist her hair. Sam tried to remember her first hour of life, holding her against his bare chest while Laura was in the recovery room, watching Lucy's eyes open to the world for the first time, examining the tiny nails and lashes of new life. He knew Lucy could only see a short distance then, and only in shadowy outlines, yet she'd seemed to take in him and every flood-lit atom of the room, weighing all of it from some timeless perspective. He remembered wondering what chance or design had thrown them together. It was humbling, a treasure.

The idyllic memory suddenly distorted. In its place appeared Clyde in his nylon golf shirt. No one at school knew how Clyde had fared since his removal. Sam was expected to know, yet he'd cut off contact with his friend. It took mere weeks before Clyde's name stopped coming up in water cooler conversation. Tidy, as though he'd never existed. And Sam didn't introduce the topic. In Sam's mind Clyde was very present. Sam woke up on the couch. It was still light out. Laura and the kids were asleep, so he walked to The Shag.

October had begun with a cold snap. The harbour was empty with the boats in dry dock. Sam ordered a cider, took a stool by the window. A group of children shuffled through a pile of leaves near the edge of the sidewalk. The smallest, a toddler, was in a Halloween mask that reminded Sam of Matthew at around the same age in his dragon costume, tripping on the rubber feet and tossing his head to realign the holes in the mask with his eyes. It started to snow. Small, light flakes. Sam watched the scene for what felt like hours. Scattered leaves gathered into eddies, twisted and dispersed.

Part Two: The Sticker Book

"Mom, can I get the Suzy Sunshine sticker book? You promised." Charla shook her mom's heavy hand, which dangled inanimately like a prosthetic at her side. Melinda had been reading the headlines of tabloid scandal at the checkout.

"Another time. Stop askin' me." Melinda filled the space on the conveyor with four tins of beans, a package of diet drink crystals, a five kilogram sack of rice, a jar of peanut butter, two loaves of bread, a box of frozen cod, and toiletries. Simple food again this week. With ample seasoning and one indulgence, a cookie or slice of pie, Melinda's dinners were appetizing. She made the most of a meager pantry. A few hearty dinners made the usual filler — mac and cheese, beans on toast, hot dogs — less objectionable. "I've enough for meals and transit 'til Thursday." She fluffed Charla's hair.

"Okay Mom." Charla didn't really care about the book itself. What mattered was Delia and the girls in her class thinking she had one. "Your momma didn't buy you a sticker book. You're a liar," Delia had said. But Charla was committed to joining the girls at the classroom window and making a show of the book's glossy pages. When Melinda said she had no money, she wasn't exaggerating to teach her daughter a lesson. There was no change tucked away in a sock drawer. That she needed it for groceries was explanation enough for Charla. The sticker book could wait.

Charla's friend Delia lived two floors down from Charla in a 60's prefab apartment. Her family was better off than Charla's — slightly. Melinda worked for a catering company; Delia's mom was a receptionist. Delia's dad drove a taxi; Charla didn't have a dad — one who was around, anyway. Charla remembered Al's quiet patter in the apartment after he got home from work. When she woke up he was already on the bus to the tailors to hem and patch, to get another season of wear out of old jackets and pants. He'd been a featureless outline in her home, an inarticulate voice.

One morning Al had ridden the bus past his stop for work to the town line. He transferred to a bus in the next town and rode it to the end of the route, then caught another bus, leapfrogging systems until nightfall, when he checked into a room with monthly rates. He'd left a sticky note on the fridge at home, the words "for the best" written in a weak scrawl.

Charla and her mom divvied up the groceries and walked through the slushy lot to the bus stop. Charla braced her chapped hands in her pockets, letting the bags dangle at her elbows. Her down-filled coat, flattened from dampness and overuse, had lost its heat-trapping properties. She wore three layers over her shirt. The covered part of her bathed in sweat while her exposed skin burned from the cold. The bus was late — or they'd missed it. Charla tapped her feet. Melinda hummed pop hits. On warmer days they'd walk to the One-Stop Shop and bus it back. By bus or foot, shopping took hours.

Charla walked to school with Delia and Melanie, friends from earliest memory. Delia was the trio's spokeswoman, a title earned in verbal spars with neighborhood bullies. New arrivals to the Merchant Street complexes — subsidized, rent assisted, or leased — soon wizened to the area's petty thievery. At this end of Ashfield car alarms were triggered by smash-and-grabs rather than mis-keyed remote controls. The bomber jackets kids wore weren't fashion statements. Looking tough paid off.

Weak-looking types were shaken down in short order.

The Evans brothers, two oversized tweens, tried to mug the girls on their way to school. Mr. Evans had lost his job at the light plant. Forced to cut back on the junk food Mom replenished weekly, the boys stuffed stolen chocolate bars up their sleeves at the grocer's. They extorted vending machine money from primary school kids, ambushed them from the recessed entrances of classrooms.

One morning Charla and the girls heard a cracking voice behind them call, "Five dollars to pass." The Evans boys had blockaded the sidewalk with dead branches which they promised to remove upon payment. Melanie, the youngest of the three girls, hid behind Charla and bawled. Delia flew into a rage: "One day you'll land in prison and daddy won't have the cash to bail you out. First thing I'm doing at school is telling the office. Might as well stay home, cuz no school is gonna take you."

The brothers hung their heads as if their mom had rebuked them. "That won't be necessary," Theo, the oldest said. "Just puttin' one by you for a laugh. Pass right on by."

Delia sapped the fight out of opponents. No offence was too petty and friends were fair game. She'd once caught Charla in a lie told to feed a conversation, a story about a fishing trip that never happened. "Who are you tryin' to impress?" Delia said. "Closest you came to fishing was pelting stones at minnows in the culvert behind the complex. Not much of a river. No rod neither." Melanie got the same star treatment. Charla didn't bother trying to defend herself. Being hypersensitive, she avoided confrontation altogether. When her mom got upset, the feeling arced through Charla. "Give 'em what they want and move on," Charla told Melanie after the Evans incident. "Those boys aren't worth a nosebleed."

For Charla there was one course, flight to safety, and no shame in taking it. "I've learned," her mom had advised her, "not to dwell. Remember the faces that hurt you, so you know them when you see them. Don't be a victim." Charla heeded the advice, even if her mom dwelled on ex-husband Al quite a bit.

Charla's friend Melanie held onto grievances. A wounded frown was her default expression. And that was the three friends together: Delia mouthing off, strutting ahead of the others; Melanie in a puffy-eyed sulk, straining back tears; and Charla, glossing over the cracks in their friendships, smiling senselessly. The girls were inseparable. Melanie's mom Sara watched Charla after school. She tried to make Charla feel welcome, but there are privileges the fairest caregivers reserve for their own children — the extra embrace after a playground bruising, the secret gift of a leftover Halloween treat.

Charla coveted Melanie's time with her stay-at-home mom. They sorted laundry and made dinner together, had the mom-daughter talk Charla waited until bedtime to have with her own mother.

Melinda tried to make up for her absence with token gestures: the promise of a long bedtime story, candy sneaked from the 'customer care bowl' on her desk at work. Her exhaustion played out in the stubbing of toes and breaking of plates as she put together a late dinner. She tried to help Charla with homework, but quickly nodded off on the couch. In turn, Charla spared her mom chores. She swept the linoleum, made breakfasts of tea and oatmeal, packed their lunches.

She also left the big jobs to her mom, to insure Melinda always felt needed. Charla wanted their time together to be stress-free, so she didn't mention the Evans boys. Each night, while rays of headlights sixteen floors down rolled across their walls, Melinda read Charla a cautionary tale, some Golden Book classic like *The Little Red Hen* from a library or yard sale. As Charla aged, the stories became more sophisticated, but they were no less instructive in their warnings against vice and misplaced trust. Charla and Melinda lay together afterwards, planned the weekend and, if they hadn't fallen asleep, asked the unanswerable questions: *How did it all begin? Does God exist? What's the purpose of life?*

And off their guards in the twilight before sleep, wondering at these mysteries, the mom-daughter roles fell away. They were just two muddlers whose paths had briefly crossed. Then Charla asked the question that was always top of mind: "Do you still think about Al?"

———————

Between the complex buildings was a wide expanse of tamped earth that dusted up in summer and oozed with gritty run-off the rest of the year. The grounds were empty but for a rusty swing set from which bored teenagers had pried the swings. In late winter snow coated the pocked surface of the grounds, making the icy crags hard to navigate on foot.

Charla's building smelled soupy and dank. The corridor walls were yellow with oven vapour and nicotine. Melinda still preferred their tired rental building to the assisted housing across the street. "I pay my way," she told Charla. There'd be more money if Melinda accessed the food bank or freebees from the Community Centre. Friends earning more than she did carted non-perishables to the complex. The thought of Charla seeing her with a hamper was enough deterrence. She'd rather buy dollar-store noodles and drink crystals than resort to charity. Charla mustn't think them desperate. The suppression of information failed. Charla was constantly aware of their poverty. The trick was hiding it from her classmates.

Melinda combed the extra small and plus-sized remainders of discontinued clothes racks for bargains. They used to shop in a small grocer's nearby. The neighboring salon in the plaza was a town hall of local characters.

Charla hammed it up when Beyoncé came on the radio, lip-sinking for an audience captive under hair dryers and tinfoil wraps. Now both the shopping and hair treatments were done at the One-Stop. Charla pulled her mom away from the racks of clothes with unfamiliar logos, hallmarks, she thought, of low budget status. The square-haired, obese women sifting through lines of unisex, universal fits, repulsed Charla. She couldn't help thinking that One-Stop customers didn't look after themselves. The unremarkable models pictured on department signs labelled 'Coats,' 'Lingerie,' 'Evening Wear' signaled mediocrity. What did that make loyal customers like her and Melinda?

When Charla heard about classmates' weekend trips to farms and conservation areas, she wondered what barred her and Melinda from the modest adventures other kids enjoyed. There were too few exceptions to their austerity. If Charla couldn't have a sticker book, a vending machine ring would've sufficed. Nothing seemed too cheap to be out of reach.

It was at the One-Stop, searching bookracks while Melinda fussed with outfits that Charla found it: *Suzy Sunshine Goes to School.* The sticker book opened with Suzy and her perfectly-proportioned friends arriving back from the beach to change into 'fab evening wear.' On TV Suzy coasted through life with sass and a smile. Her problems were cute and solvable. Had Suzy's mom ever failed to make rent? Questions of affordability never came up. Suzy was too busy singing to packed halls or snaring a beau for the school dance. She didn't have to be funny or clever to win attention. Canned laughter came on cue at the end of each scene.

At school Charla flipped through old fashion magazines that her class used to make collages. The tall, slender models weren't like the people she knew: odalisque figures in over-sized belts and scarves with handbags too small to hold a wallet. Melinda had a heart-shaped pendant from her grandmother that she kept in a box with plastic costume jewelry. As a toddler Charla pranced through the apartment layered with necklaces. The clunky beads draped below her chubby knees and snagged the corners of tables. She remembered Al calling her his "Nubian princess." Was that why she liked costume jewelry?

On Saturday morning Melanie and Delia visited Charla while Melinda slept. They turned the hall into a runway that they strutted in her mom's old dresses and camisoles. The washroom became a dressing room complete with broken lipstick tubes and rusty compacts reclaimed from the backs of dresser drawers. They cooled off on the balcony, watched shoppers in Merchant Street below, searched for sailboats in Old Ashfield Harbour.

———————

The bus pulled up and Charla ran to the door. "Slow down," said Melinda. "I'm coming too you know." She ripped a square off the sheet of bus tokens and passed it to Charla. Something pent-up was about to erupt. Charla knew when to back off.

Melinda had thought herself adaptable in a crisis, the sort who could change house and job on short notice. When Al hadn't come home from work by the weekend, she'd needed someone to confide in. The women on her floor had gathered in the hall before dinner to vent about their day. Melinda turned to Sara: "Al's gone. I don't expect him back."

"What are you going to do?" Sara had said.

"Why should *I* change a thing? I didn't leave." Melinda stayed with Charla in the matrimonial apartment and kept her entry level job. The loss of Al's income was a swift downgrade. Who plans to be left? Melinda wanted Charla to hold her own at school, to take her daughter to a restaurant once a year where food isn't served on plastic trays, to put her in an after school program.

They became do-it-yourselfers, learned to cook from scratch, stitch outfits from patterns, clip coupons, enter giveaways. There was no burning through savings on a devil-may-care afternoon buying the clothes they wanted instead of what they could afford.

Charla's social life was limited by the price of participation. For friends' birthdays she bought knock-off dollar store gifts. On school trips she ate squashed sandwiches while classmates lined up for food court pizza. The grade eight Quebec trip that her classmates waited all of elementary school to attend was a forgone conclusion: She wouldn't go.

"Sorry, I didn't mean to rush," Charla said. She walked back to Melinda so they could board the bus in lockstep.

Melinda stared out the window, her cheer at the One Stop given way to an inlaid gloom. She watched the muddy snowbanks and terrace housing pass on the wide road. The street was thick with brownish-grey, half-frozen sludge, the sky overcast. Melinda had been remote before. Now her face had a rooted quality that scared Charla. It would be harder to bring her mom back this time.

"Mom, next stop is ours." She tapped Melinda's shoulder and took grocery bags off of the bench, wishing she didn't have to be the one to take charge. Charla had her own dreams, which she indulged when Mom went to bed. The apartment's heat was centrally programmed by property management at a high temperature that made blankets superfluous, so Charla left her window open. As she slept, the cool current made her feel encamped on the shore of a northern lake. A siren or tire squeal stirred her, or that sound that visited with heartbeat regularity: the horn of the freight train. Its baritone droned in and out of the background, marking time like a celestial clock. Late at night, after the village emptied of traffic and voices, the horn broke through walls and into dreams. For her mom, who'd lived her life under its watch, the sound was a constant, from a train in a valley she'd never seen, a vestige of lumber yards and forests on the northern frontier. On hearing it, Charla smelled pine saps and the iron scent of moving water, far from the asphalt and blank walls of the complex.

Living on a peninsula between two Great Lakes, Melinda insisted Charla learn to swim. When bacteria counts fell and summer heat made hiking a chore, they day-tripped to Burlington Beach. By late September, swimming outside was a shivery, goose-pimpled affair, so Charla began lessons at an indoor pool. Melanie and Delia agreed to wait poolside twice a week, so Charla wouldn't have to walk alone to Sara's after school. Charla learned fast. She was less buoyant than her pudgier teammates and had to muscle past them, starting strokes with her bicep against her ear then extend her reach, synching to the rhythm of her breath. She gradually became relaxed in the water. Finally, something she could do better than her classmates.

Charla hadn't really talked to her mom in weeks. In the afterglow of her pool success, she'd forgotten how little Melinda's life had changed. Her mom was the face complainants greeted when they raged through the door of Customer Service. By the time they met management, Melinda had taken the flak for her superiors. She'd learned to detach herself from customer attacks, but found it increasingly hard to let down her guard at home. She'd grown distant.

At dinner Charla tried to start a conversation. *Does anything excite Mom anymore?* Melinda's idea of a good time was pretty basic: spending time with her daughter. Charla worried about the extent of her mom's reliance on her. How would Melinda would cope when Charla grew up, having no excuse of parental sacrifice to hide behind?

Melinda collapsed into bed after dinner and awoke to Charla perched at the bedside. "What is it, sweet?"

"Think you'll ever remarry, Mom?"

"Why, you think I need a husband? Someone else isn't responsible for your happiness. Happiness is a choice."

"Do I make you happy?" Charla said.

"That's different."

Her mom brushed off the suggestion of romance. She'd turned down invitations from coworkers. Melinda took refuge in her work. Colleagues embraced the version of herself that she disclosed to them.

"I want you to be happy," Charla said.

"I am happy."

"I know you're fine. You should be more than fine."

"I prefer knowing what to expect," Melinda said. She felt reckless being candid with a daughter who was still a child. Why hasten maturity? Their family life would change soon enough, Melinda knew. She relied on Charla for the support adult friends are supposed to provide. She watches Charla dress for school. Teetering on one foot while tying a shoe in her top-heavy, lopsided backpack, Charla spilled into the closet. Her goofiness rescued Melinda yet again from the constant self-examination that made it impossible for her to relax.

Unable to swim after school, Charla leaned on the arm of Melanie's sofa, fist in face, watching reruns through bad reception. By the time Melinda picked her up, Charla wanted to sleep, but she stayed up late with her mom. They were both sleep-deprived. Anyway, tomorrow was Saturday.

In the morning they slept in. Melinda cooked a heavy English breakfast and her famous corn bread, then Charla read while Melinda did small renoes: a wallpaper border for the kitchen, grouting for the bathtub. They played cards. Melinda had bought a book on two-player card games. Cribbage was last Christmas's hit. They played Rummy through March, and now whist filled their time. But Melinda wanted to take Charla outside the complex, out of Ashfield altogether. There wasn't an operational playground in the village. They'd go to a pumpkin patch or orchard, if there was a bus to take them there. So they went to the train station.

Charla examined a map of the Lakeview Line in the waiting room, pointed out landmarks within walking distance of the stations. She recognized the streets from radio and TV news, names associated with traffic delays and crime scenes. As she reeled off attractions, Melinda was struck by how small their world had become.

"If I'm under budget this week, we'll take the train next Saturday," Melinda promised. Charla couldn't wait. She borrowed sightseeing brochures from Sara, plotted routes.

The following Saturday they were on a Toronto-bound train. Charla ditched her itinerary. "Let's make this an adventure," she announced. The smells caught her attention right away, the salted fish of Kensington, hung like laundry in storefronts, the fumes of street vendors at intersections: buttery caramel, baked pretzel, chili sausage. Charla loved the bombastic commercialism of Yonge Street, the Victorian boutiques of Queen West. They walked all day. High and low, neighborhoods held together in a way Ashfield didn't. In its disorderliness, the city had struck a balance. Her complex was a scar on Ashfield's otherwise perfect skin. Charla knew but didn't speak of the difference between their corner of Merchant Street and the rest of Ashfield. Why should she feel ashamed? In Kensington there was too much squalor to be phased by it. Walking a block was a trip from Brazil to Jamaica to Ethiopia. Variety ruled. How often had she walked in

Ashfield and thought, *Why do so few people look like me?*

They took the Toronto Island ferry. It might as well have been a four-star cruise. Charla watched the towering skyline recede from the stern. She'd never boarded a boat she didn't have to paddle. It couldn't be real, the car-free cottage roads on Ward's Island, a stone's throw from skyscrapers. They ate packed lunches on the beach, watched the sunset reflected on glass and steel.

On each subsequent trip downtown, they visited a different attraction: Royal Ontario Museum, Hockey Hall of Fame, Science Centre, Art Gallery of Ontario.

Melinda hadn't been to the art gallery since she was a kid. She remembered the Rothko painting, still hung in the foyer, three streaks of colour that her teacher had called "botched graffiti." She'd avoided galleries when Charla was younger, afraid the child would maul the silicon baby head or chicken in a suit installations.

The swing in form and subject on the white walls – from an oil of a Roman ruin to a silkscreen of an airport terminal to a photo of a garbage-filled Yangtze River – disorientated Charla. She felt displaced yet renewed and tried to recreate the experience after they left the gallery. She bought a notebook in a gift shop. They stopped in a café. A song on the sound system sparked a train of thought she couldn't get down on paper fast enough. She tore pictures of models and world leaders out of discarded newspapers, attached headlines from articles, worked in dialogue, added frames and captions. Her comics were social commentary.

The train trips had served Melinda's purpose. Charla was becoming more conscious and discerning of her world. She began to read voraciously, borrowed library books that explained events she'd seen in art, histories intended for older readership: Gibbons' *The Decline and Fall of the Roman Empire*, Ovid's *Metamorphosis*. Paintings like "The Massacre of the Innocents" and "The Assassination of Caesar" depicted a dark humanity. She wondered what other horrors she'd been spared.

Her school created book dioramas and announcements for Black History Month. Every year she reeled off factoids to Delia and

Melanie about Rosa Parks, Martin Luther King, Hariet Tubman, figuring she had the key figures and their accomplishments committed to memory. Then she stumbled across Siebert's *Underground Railroad from Slavery to Freedom* at the library. She took the book from the display case and spent the Sunday afternoon in a window nook poring over it. Melinda was making her own discoveries and only too happy to hear her daughter asking questions: How had slavery wounded her ancestors? How hard won were the battles of the Civil Rights movement? Why was so little of it memorialized in art? The depictions of Greco-Roman demi-gods and the descendants of Biblical Adam in galleries and museums were endless, but what of her ancestry in East Africa? Histories of the Ethiopian empire were hard to find. Charla's research exposed a troubling pattern: the underrepresentation of her people.

She reflected in her notebook. Writing sharpened her opinions, made them powerful and terse. Melinda hadn't expected Charla to communicate with such authority, and she didn't realize how much her own life had changed.

As a child Melinda was an average artist, mocked and faintly praised like most of her classmates. By grade eight she'd stopped drawing for pleasure. Why was she suddenly drawn to painting?

When her washer broke down and she had to use the Merchant Street Launderette, she noticed a small lithograph on the faded plaster wall of Conception Bay, Newfoundland: Through a narrow gap in the low clouds, rays of light illuminated a patch of rough sea. The artist depicted the bay as a magnetic v-birth pulling ships into its field, as though nature had ordained St. John's centre of the hemisphere. Melinda had passed her life within a mile of this launderette, spent full afternoons in the long soporific white room. Why hadn't she noticed that scene? The picture transported her from the village like a portal. She felt like she was on that cliff watching the sky and boats shift, and she wondered what else art could do for her.

She borrowed books on landscape artists, all British and dead: Gainsborough, Constable, Turner. She explored art forms and movements from medieval triptychs to twentieth century Futurism. The European portraits of patrons were fussy and self-important, not at all the people she knew. The later French and Dutch painters captured feeling, as if the camera-eye view of the world missed the point. Simple subjects — dancers, haystacks, chairs — quaked with life, fluid objects, frozen on canvas before morphing into something else.

She read about abstract art, studied the Mondrian squares and the Pollock drips, the why of their placement in the pantheon of great art. But it was the nature scenes that held her attention, the swaths of red and yellow leaves in Algoma Canyon, the blue icebergs off Ellesmere Island. She also studied the art of her ancestry, saw her features in the slender figurines, but she'd spent her life in Canada. Ethiopia wasn't her experience.

Lauren Harris's scenes of northern Canada fifty years ago made her want to paint. In a dozen hues and shapes, he captured the essence of an Arctic sunset. Abstract and concrete, charged with feeling and remote, rising and dying in a cycle.

Charla screamed, "Mom!" The machinery upriver made it hard to hear what had happened in the next room. Delia had tripped over the coffee table while the friends were playing tag. Melinda dabbed the cut with a cloth. The complex wasn't conducive to play or mental work. Outside noise pierced thoughts and made readers lose their places on pages.

Melinda wanted to go north, take the Polar Bear Express to James Bay and explore – or if she couldn't get there, experience the country through art. For so long she'd felt ordinary. *Wash and wear.* Even the local Merchant Street college students in their thrift shop, hand-altered clothes managed to have style. Their clipper cropped hair looked avant-garde. Did they have more money than she did? What kept her from being that resourceful? Her next pair of glasses would be horn-rimmed, her next hairdo, angular.

She remembered art in grade school being an afterthought crammed in between the *important* subjects. She never had time to do her best. Some make-work task – copying a board note she could've been given in a handout – cut her short. Some kids took private art classes. Compared to Melinda's works, scratched on paper with stumpy pencil crayons, theirs were technical marvels: rooflines tapered to vanishing points in true perspective; colours joined at the seam without bleeding together.

Melinda couldn't afford art lessons for herself while Charla swam competitively.

Anyway, she wanted to be with Charla at night. Apart from the confrontations with customers and the juicy confidences of coworkers, Melinda's job was tedious. People's problems were often self-made, the fruit of scheming, unimaginative minds. She'd caved into her worst instincts and gotten swept up in their melodramas.

Melinda entered an art supply store she'd passed by her whole life without a thought to its contents.

"Where'd you get those?" Charla asked.

"On our street." Melinda emptied her bags on the kitchen table while Charla looked on from the couch. If the purchases weren't gifts, Charla wanted to witness this strange event.

Melinda squeezed tubes of acrylic paint onto a disk and mixed colours. Enlisting books on technique, she practiced fundamentals: dry brush stroke, dappling, shading for depth and shadow. After gaining control of line, she focused on colour. Transitions were tough: the move from cerulean blue to pale turquoise in a twilit sky. But it was solid colours – the single, unchanging tone in a leaf from petiole to apex

– that sapped her as she touched and retouched the canvas.

She painted while dinner cooked, losing track of time and washing her brushes while Charla pretended to enjoy a charred meal.

Melinda painted every day. As the sessions gained intensity she lost patience with the complex. "I can't handle the air in here."

"Why not paint outdoors?" Charla said.

On an April Saturday, Melinda packed paints and pine panels, dropped Charla at Sara's, and hiked six miles north of town. She climbed a rickety staircase up the face of Rattlesnake Point and set her panels on a billions year-old Silurian rock outcrop. She imagined herself an explorer.

On the gravel shoulders of one-lane regional roads, she looked down the driveways of farms and old logging trails for a deserted site to occupy, for artifacts of a once thriving way of life: plank barns, rusted steel silos, mud-floor cellars, grinding stones, oxidized tractors. Not much at first glance, but in the grainy slats of petrified wood and rotted foundations were timeless images. She felt like she'd been here before. Thick bands of blue-black raincloud swept in from the west, perforated by clear rays of orange light. A blue haze transfigured the woodlots, as if a spirit possessed them.

She tried to paint the faraway places that she couldn't visit using photos found online at work. But each photo was a piece of art all its own. Deciding that someone else's vision shouldn't form the basis of her work, she discarded the photos and painted from imagination. Did any place look the way she'd imagined it? No place looks the same way twice, she thought, remembering Monet's studies of haystacks at different times of day and year: the shaded earth tones of late-day fall, the pastels of midday spring. She painted the places she wanted to visit so she could inhabit them through art.

Charla asked, "Why don't you paint a European village or mythological scene like the ones in your books?"

"Nature's harder," Melinda said. She wanted to travel. She and Al had talked about renting a cottage. Melinda usually took her vacation in the off season so coworkers could take theirs in summer. This year she took it at peak season.

Melinda rented a cabin at Turkey Point on Lake Erie. The cottagers next door came for a month each summer. Charla and Melinda only had a week, but they'd gotten a taste of cottage life. Charla looked for snakes in the tall grass. Melinda set her easel on the front porch. The trip confirmed Charla's suspicion: It's a different world for those with means. "Enjoy it," Melinda told her, "You may not come back this way again." Charla assumed she wouldn't.

Returning home was hard. Ashfield was built over two centuries, laid out south to north on a descending scale of property value. The complex was a low income housing initiative, its narrow strip of land cinched between a tannery and rail line on the north edge of town, long the target of town planners who'd rather a slab be erected where industrial waste had tarred the soil.

The towers had a forlorn beauty. Melinda couldn't bring herself to paint them. Too familiar, too stark. Its industrial neighbours were a common grievance of Merchant Street tenants. The mill clattered until nightfall. A foggy stench from the sewage treatment plant downriver wafted up the valley and settled between the towers. An area that was undesirable to begin with was easily neglected. Land values were low, the tax base starved. Walkways were cracked and discoloured by effluent from the tannery. Not a stone had been replaced since the sidewalk was laid. Street cleaners bypassed the complex's inner network of roads on their nightly rounds. The street furniture and greenery of Main Street, its brimming flower baskets and old-worldy cast-iron light standards, were unimaginable here. No advocacy group proposed them. Residents who demanded better ran afoul of Ashfield's power brokers.

Against the odds, the Merchant Street Business Improvement Association persuaded Council to install police in the park at night and hire city workers to clear garbage once a week.

As long as Main Street and Merchant Village were separated by fields, the property values in Old Ashfield remained unsullied and those who benefitted from the current arrangement saw no reason, save a moral one, to change it. When the two burgeoning wards grew into one another, town tabloid editor

Dickie Turner called for an end to the encroachment of the "northern slum." Freezing development wouldn't be easy, but Old Ashfield's resident associations had friends on Council and an army of Boomer volunteers freshly retired from Bay Street banks.

The disparity of services between the two wards was impossible to ignore. Without prominence of name or position, the Merchant Street Business Association wrote letters, petitioned Council, knocked on doors. Melinda couldn't decide whether fortune had smiled on the village or if this was a last gasp of activism in a losing war.

Charla asked questions Melinda couldn't answer. "Why isn't there a park here? I have to press a leaf in wax paper for Science. There isn't a tree in the complex."

She told Charla about segregation in the South and Apartheid in South Africa, but Charla already knew the history, and wasn't their predicament more about class than racial divide? She was more learned than Melinda was at her age, and more determined not to be held back by history.

Her confidence wavered when a note arrived at school saying Melinda would be home early, that Charla should skip swimming and go straight to Melanie's. Charla rocked herself on Melanie's couch. "Mom never comes home early," she told Melanie, who proceeded to loan Charla her Suzy Sunshine sticker book with costume cut-outs. Sara tried calling Melinda at work for answers, but she'd already left for the day.

Charla was asleep when Melinda finally arrived. She carried her daughter's dense swimmer's body to bed.

Charla woke with a start in the night. A light was on in the living room. She found Melinda reading a letter. Melinda scanned the note longer than it took to read it. "What is it?" Charla said. She should've been deep in REM sleep, out cold. Melinda opened her mouth, then thought better of speech, handing Charla the wrinkled note instead.

Dear Melinda,

Nothing I can say will explain why I left. You don't know how badly I've wanted to see you and Charla all these years. I'm sorry I haven't sent you any money. I can't say where I am.

Please don't try looking for me. Tell Charla I love her.

Al

Charla expected to feel curious about Al's situation and pleased that Dad had made contact, yet his apology rang hollow. The note interfered with the self-sufficiency she and her mom had learned by necessity after Al absconded. Or was that his point, to stir feelings that prevented them from moving on?

Charla had been waiting to hear from him. In the seconds it took to read his note, she lost interest in his plight and whatever personal need had taken him away in the first place. How important was she to him? How dare he think a note could begin to compensate for missing her formative years?

Melinda switched off the light. They fell asleep together on the living room couch.

Charla had a supply teacher the next day, Miss Roto. The retired substitute juddered over the attendance: "Charles Dean"

"Here."

"Christie *Bog-nas* — sorry — *Bon-yas*."

"Here."

"Charla Stephenson." Charla was watching the picture of the Queen and the seconds hand on the clock above the blackboard.

"Charla Stephenson," the teacher repeated. Delia swatted Charla in the back of the head. Charla pricked up like a startled cat. "Prime Minister Stephen Harper," the teacher said. Chuckles issued from the back of the room.

"Here," Charla said. She was daydreaming, not about Al, but a world without deadbeat dads and droning teachers. Charla's imagination had been erupting. During French and math, heroes and villains from the legends she read at night dueled between the desks. She imagined hunting magic relics in a school hallway besieged by half-blood dragons. Her school had become enchanted. Her desk was a caravan on an ancient dessert pass.

Not wanting to appear antisocial or superior, Charla restricted her reading at Melanie's to school textbooks. Charla's friends didn't share her passion for books. Delia was chatty and impulsive. Melanie's parents forbid the thrillers that would've interested their daughter. So Charla waited until the weekend to immerse herself in Narnia or Wonderland. Through books she could leave Ashfield without getting off the couch.

Suzy Sunshine cut a poor figure next to *Dr. Jekyll* or *Sir Gawain*. When one book ended Charla began the next as though the same story continued under a new cover.

As far back as Charla could recall, she and her mom had felt they'd missed out. There was a party somewhere else to which they weren't invited, and any place was better than the complex. No longer. Home was a source of strength. Between sittings at the canvas, Melinda explained a new work, why she chose that emerald for the sky, where she'd seen it one twilight. Charla talked about her latest read. The themes in her reading had gotten harder. Characters' problems had no clear solutions. Children's books had tidier endings.

Charla began to wonder if reading was a substitute for living. And was her mom hiding from life behind art? Escapism crashed into reality at school. Charla's classmates were better this year at distinguishing the brand names from the knock-offs. Melinda had prided herself on finding bargain clothes that looked like popular brands. The cuts matched the original designs, but the colours faded and the threads worked loose from the lower-grade cloth. If Charla wore a new shirt to school, kids made a point of asking where she got it, knowing full well it came from The One-Stop.

When the three friends got to the playground on Monday, Delia ran off to play hopscotch. Melanie trailed close behind. Charla sat on her backpack against the wall and opened up Morley Callaghan's *Luke Baldwin's Vow,* the story of a boy who, after being orphaned, has to move to another town to live with his uncle.

A ball from a nearby game of handball flew into Charla's ear. "Aaah!" She ducked, cupped her hand over the sting. The bell rang. Students lined up in rows. Zach, one of the students who might've thrown the ball — might've thrown it on purpose — grabbed the lapel of Charla's faded jacket. "You still wearin' velcro? Velcro girl!" he shouted. He ripped apart the straps fastening her jacket. A group of older students circled Charla. Some laughed and pointed. Others just watched, saying nothing. Melanie was out of earshot in another line.

Delia, distracted by her own loud line, couldn't hear Charla cry, "Don't touch me!"

"What? I'm only teasing," Zach said. Charla thought better of arguing. He'd use anything she said to paint her as a suck. Then life as she knew it would be over. So she let the matter slide.

On schedule, the horn of the train echoed through the playground. Her class entered the heavy double doors. At recess, when students brought out their toys and handheld gadgets, Charla hid her library book. She waited until silent reading to dig it out of her backpack, imagining for now that she was above the video games and sticker books that the other girls showed off. But no one noticed her uppity stance, and she succumbed to the craven old habit of coveting their stuff. She wanted a sticker book.

The day wouldn't end. She had to calculate the cost of retiling and repainting her classroom. The multi-step problem required she measure room dimensions, convert metric units, calculate surface area, multiply decimal dollar amounts. Charla stared out the window at the green field and thought about swimming. Would Delia and Melanie wait for her at the pool today? Monday wasn't on the schedule they'd agreed to. Wouldn't it be easier on everyone, she thought, if Mom let her walk home alone after school? Child safety precautions seemed excessive. Didn't her mom ride the bus by herself as a kid? What kind of world was it that she couldn't return a library book on her own without fear of abduction? She felt smothered, from a distance, since Melinda wasn't there to check up on her. All the same, Charla kept her word, bypassing the rec centre with Delia and Melanie on the way home.

At Melanie's she restrained herself from reading her book. The 60-year-old *Luke Baldwin's Vow* still held up. She understood Luke's loneliness after his father died, this permanent exile of having to live with his uncle. Did he feel stuck like she did in Melanie's apartment? The ragged toys, the inscrutable homework, the attention to Melanie's trite personal dramas, but most of all the waiting to get home, where she could be herself with her mom. What made Delia and Melanie friends? She loved them like family, yet weren't they friends of convenience? It served them to walk to school together. Melinda said even good friends grow apart. Charla hadn't believed her until now.

Melinda had stayed up painting the night before and wanted to continue, so Charla read. After dinner there was an unfamiliar knock at the door. Sellers sometimes sneaked into the building, ignoring the eye-level 'No Solicitors' sign in the entrance. They followed residents in, grabbed the door before it shut, lied about the purpose of their visit: "I forgot my friend's buzz code."

Melinda looked through the peephole at a youngish man in a navy suit. She opened the door expecting to see a vacuum nearby with attachments, a salesman's demo kit. Instead, a stack of pictures was on the floor, lithographs of idyllic winter scenes: kids decorating a snowman in a public square, families skating on a pond behind a century home. Deeper in the pile were East Coast scenes of rocky shores and fishermen rowing bright-hued dories. A red clay island in the Gulf of St. Laurence made Melinda gasp.

"I want to show you something," Melinda told the man. Richard was his name. He was averse to small talk, having heard enough tire-kickers. Richard would rather the door were slammed in his face than listen to people with no intent to buy wax poetic about art. He had a pitch that sold — if he got a chance to deliver it. Business was brisk.

Something plaintive in Melinda's voice made him drop his pitch and follow her inside. On the kitchen table was a maritime scene almost identical to the one he'd shown her. That she'd painted the same island didn't seem implausible — she might've summered there — until he learned she'd never seen it. And her imagined version had the one he peddled beat. Richard inspected the canvas, "Where do you sell your work?"

"I haven't thought of selling it," Melinda said.

"You should think about that." Through Richard's eyes Charla saw the work anew. She thought her mom painted well, but hadn't considered just how well. Talent didn't come into why she supported Mom's painting. Art took the edge off of Melinda, this venom she carried and sometimes unleashed on Charla. But wasn't Melinda a hack who'd amount to a folk hero at best, a community mascot, the 'wack job' on the sixteenth floor? The evidence was on the table. Next to the other artists' works, Melinda's mastery was undeniable. Charla felt witness to a watershed in her mom's life.

"What's involved in exhibiting art?" Melinda said.

"Not to worry," Richard said. "I know some gallery owners." He envied art dealers with the foresight to back unknowns whose best years lay ahead, but he was a novice appraiser, pushing mass-produced prints to a market that cared little about art. "I know people who'd buy your work." Browsing through the heaps of Melinda's paintings, he seized upon one of a decaying barn. "I could take your work on consignment, see what happens."

"What's consignment?" Charla said.

Melinda took Charla's hand. "I'm only paid if they sell."

"Sounds fair," Charla said.

Melinda took Richard's business card. That night she tallied her works — thirty-seven, a prolific year for any artist, and the year wasn't over. A fire burned under her that week and into the next. "I don't know if I'm ready," Melinda said. "I'm still learning to paint."

"You'll always be learning," Charla said.

Melinda had practiced so much already – transitioning from dark to light, layering and stippling paint to build texture, setting colours beside each other that blended from afar. She played with composition, shifted the relative positions of figures, birches and pines jutting out of shallow stone crevices, islands of granite and quartz in the Canadian Shield. She finally understood technical terms, could produce the effects, yet she was unsure of herself. How skilled was she? Knowing the recipe – which ingredients and how much of each to apply – was where the mastery lay. The moment of creation, where infinite choices are made in the stroke of a brush, was an act for which there could be no guidebook.

So she challenged herself, drew the objects that amateurs avoid: faces, hands, anatomy. She studied the Golden Ratio of part to whole, the Divine Proportion of natural phenomena, the distances between points on a leaf, digits on a finger. She drew Charla's face from memory, reviewed it as though it was a last extant photo. Before putting paint to canvas, Melinda made a series of sketches, as a Great Master lays the groundwork for the final *pièce de resistance.*

If she feared that painting made her a less attentive parent, Melinda also believed she was modeling a prized character trait: passion for life. Charla was following her interests and nurturing her talents, yet this too scared Melinda. Soon the draw of somewhere or someone else would prove irresistible and Charla would leave. Painting calmed Melinda's fears. Selling her work seemed the next logical step.

There was no more space in the spare room for pictures. The spoils of swim meets choked the walls: badges, ribbons, plaques, team photos. Melinda hesitated to give paintings to friends who mightn't appreciate them but hang them out of obligation. Family was different — or should be, she thought. Melinda had kept Charla's infant scribbles. They were connections through time. Certain her own mother would feel the same way, Melinda brought her a painting.

Alicia was no ordinary mom or grandmother. Her rap list of public mischief was long and growing. On an unscheduled visit to the doctor with a five year-old Melinda, Alicia had demanded immediate attention for a neck rash and strong-armed the secretary into a room where the doctor was seeing a patient. Police had to escort mom and daughter off the property.

Alicia was irritated by people who were merely getting on with their lives — lining up to buy license plate stickers, shoveling walkways, taking out the recycling.

Melinda dutifully visited "Granny" twice a month, getting her groceries, renewing her prescriptions, taking her to the spa for pick-me-up pedicures. If not for Melinda's check-ins, Alicia wouldn't have visitors. For her good deeds Melinda was rewarded with criticism. Today was no exception. She handed Alicia a painting of the stream they frequented when Melinda was a child. Alicia tossed it across the counter like another prescription. "You look tired," Alicia said. "Why not put on some makeup and find yourself a man?"

Charla set aside her favourite works-by-mom. Melinda had her pick five to give Richard to sell. Charla liked the local disused barns that Melinda thought poor substitutes for the seaside bluffs and fishing villages they couldn't visit out East. She saw a pattern in the sagging barns and solitary sheds, imagining Melinda sitting cross-legged in the foreground, in a field as abandoned as Al had made them feel.

————————

As they waited on the platform, Charla pasted the "Polar Bear Express" brochure into a sketchpad-journal stuffed to bursting with daytrip mementos. On the way to this northernmost Ontario highway they'd canoed Red River rapids and waded waste-deep through Prince Edward County marsh to sketch irises. From here only railway and wilderness.

Northern Ontario might've been another continent: Forests of knobby firs stretched to infinity. Flocks of godwit shorebirds scavenged the beaches of James Bay. A cree hunting party tore through the lands of an 18th century trading post in a monster pick-up. Charla and Melinda rented a canoe and paddled the Moose River until their arms gave out. The night sky came alive at new moon, the rust belt light pollution a thousand kilometres removed. They watched the starlight from their sleeping bags, the only man-made object a satellite on a fixed path. An angler gave Charla and Melinda trout, which they roasted over fire as the temperature plummeted. Between encampments, they portaged and rowed – and talked when it became too tranquil.

All five paintings sold. The barns went first. Her one mural, a wall-sized ninety by eighty inches, paid for their northern trip. The buyer said the landscape reminded her of a farm she'd lived that had been expropriated to build a toll highway.

Melinda had splurged on train tickets and camping gear. James Bay was the farthest she'd been from Ashfield. Slashing through underbrush with kit on her back, following the custom of the Canadian artist-adventurer, she'd canoed to remote riverbeds, set up her easel on clods of earth to get the perfect sightline. On days off, she couldn't leave home without the kit. A day without painting was a privation. Art had raised their living standards. She hadn't quit her job, but who knew what lay ahead? So much had changed already.

––––––––––––

They settled into their cabin on the northbound train. Melinda passed a purple package to Charla. Inside she expected to find more of the dog-eared paperbacks that made their rounds in the apartment before being re-traded for more used books. But these had a film on the covers and drooped like magazines. They smelled sugary and chemical, as though the ink hadn't dried. *Suzy Sunshine* sticker books. Charla nuzzled her mom's arm and opened a book, rubbed the tacky pages between her fingers, tore off the cellophane sticker sheet.

The fuss was for her mom's benefit. Charla didn't say it, but she'd lost interest in sticker books. Part of her couldn't wait to bring them to school and indulge in the kind of gloating she'd endured since kindergarten. She felt so different from the other kids. Wouldn't the books make her more comprehensible to classmates than the novels she skulked away to read at her desk?

Class approval didn't mean what it used to. And worrying less what people thought seemed to wipe the target off of her forehead. Her newfound independence disarmed Zach and the Evans brothers, who circumvented her on the sidewalk like rivulets around a rock.

Mom's art sales insured that Charla would attend that graduation trip to Quebec City. No more of the tight-fisted compromise associated with admission costs.

Perhaps the biggest assurance came from the change in Melinda's painting. Her subjects had become less solitary. Charla remembered when the shift happened. They were canoeing in Algonquin Provincial Park. Melinda paddled to the shore to paint the distant tree-line. Charla was doodling in her notebook. She climbed out of the canoe, ducked under water, blew bubbles, and came up for air. Melinda forgot what she was painting and watched Charla tread water in the shallow bay. No one else was around. If Melinda wasn't there, no one would have seen her daughter, who in that moment was Melinda's entire world. And the world gave Melinda all that she asked of it. When they returned home, Melinda painted the scene from memory.

Richard came to their apartment to get a painting a collector had commissioned. He bought a painting a month from Melinda, his first steady artist as a dealer of originals. Satisfied that the scene matched the quality of her other works, he lingered in the doorway. "Have you finished anything else? Just thought I'd ask since I'm here."

Melinda got a folder from the spare room and took out several mostly unfinished paintings. He showed mild interest the first few he saw then seized on one. "Is that Charla?" The one of her treading water in the bay. "Can I take it?"

"Not that one," Melinda said.

"Too bad. I've never seen so much love in a portrait." When he left, Melinda tested the painting against different walls of the apartment, finally settling on the kitchen, where she'd spend many of the hours that remained to her. That one wasn't for sale.

Part Three: Uncommon

1

A thermal hum of maxed out audio vibrates the floor. Rows of flickering white and red light floods the stage. Silicone, Leanne's band, is almost up. She's got her head turner, a black nylon tee and red plastic mini-skirt. In the wing she holds the bass to her ear to hear past the distortion of the opening act. She imagines her first album taking off, the sea of faces crowding the stage at the new release party. Two hours ago the bar was empty. She'd lugged equipment backstage across the floor, still sticky from last night's beer. The fluorescent lights were on for cleaning — the dull ones illuminated to turf dawdlers at closing time. Leanne was another stage hand at sound check, puffy-eyed and dowdy in her sweats. The pre-show set-up, practices, hours of solitary writing — all are back-story if they put on a good show.

Her slight frame looks healthful beside the skeletons she plays with. Two hours ago the place was beyond redemption. Sometime during the opener the dingy hole became a concert hall. Guests dance in their seats at the back. Up front fans crush into the stage. A roady flicks a stage-diver into the mosh-pit.

Marley's is credited with vaulting local acts onto the international stage. The Stones played here when Keith was hauled up on heroine charges in '78. The infamous half-condemned tavern is the kind of dump bands want in the touring chapter of their unofficial biography. Autographed band photos glut the walls like plaques in a mausoleum.

Leanne watches the entrance where two doughboy bouncers in headsets stand guard. No sign of Jake. He told her he'd come. The main aisle's full. Whistles and cheers. She hopes Silicone's applause matches the opener's. Critics mean more to her than she'd care to admit, the chance they'd cast her as an Indi wannabe. She tunes her base, mutters, "Four years of playing with that egomaniac Nathan and his layabout sidekick."

Sandra and Victoria come backstage, friends from art school. They design sets. Leanne's Plan B if the dream sours. "Thanks for coming." Leanne swoons to hug them. They wish her well. Sandra and Vic come to every show. She's begun to wonder if they're waiting for her to fail. "Still making sets for the Carmen production, Vic?" Leanne says.

"Yeah. I've decided I hate opera."

"I see how that might happen," Leanne says, stumped. What's left to say if set design, their one shared interest, is off limits? She says to Sandra, "Tony's upstairs doing sound for Scunner. Go up. I'm sure he can talk." She's here to see him anyway, Leanne thinks. *Piss off.*

She waits for the rest of Silicone to arrive. "I'm always the first one here, setting up their shit," Leanne says.

Sandra sneaks up behind Tony on the landing, plants a hand on his back. His eyes don't leave the mixing board. Sandra might fit into his bigger picture one day, but not now, not until Silicone gets mainstream airplay.

"When are you up?" Sandra says.

"After them," Tony says. "One or two more songs. Not bad, eh? Sort of Celtic. Real East Coast ceilidh music. We might do more shows together. See the suit in the mullet down there? Sony Music's A & R guy. I don't know if he's here for them or us."

"Wow," she says. She'd lavish praise on him, but this isn't the time to blow smoke. A record deal could really happen. *Best not get his hopes up.* Silicone's gathering momentum. Their self-published CD posted record hits on MySpace last month. *Here*, the nightlife city tabloid, ran a half-page feature with glowing endorsements of the band from alt-rock hitmakers, Shrinkwrap.

"Yup, a big show tonight," Tony says. "If we get a deal I'll move out of the crawlspace."

Tony rents a nook at the end of a narrow attic. The legal tenants sublet it to him behind the landlord's back. The windowless landing is a firetrap. His safety plan is an expired hand-sized extinguisher.

Nathan comes into the booth. "Two more songs then it's us. We're pretty much set." He shouts across the booth at Sandra, so Tony doesn't miss a word, "How's working with thespians?"

"I hide with the set crew behind the scenes. We build sets while the actors pretend to rehearse. What a ragged bunch. We find them under stage props, sleeping and screwing each other," Sandra says. Nathan's eyes track Tony's fingers on the mixing board. Sandra casts around for an audience, but no one is paying attention.

She suspects Nathan only talks to her in deference to Tony. She's right. Tony holds one speaker of the headset to his ear, adjusts the mixer with his other hand. He adds reverb to the hardest vocal parts, raises the distortion on the fret-tapping solos, causing the 16th notes to blear together so the guitarist's mistakes go unnoticed. Tony's work doesn't make or break a show. That's up to the band. If they loosen up, so does the audience. Errors are forgotten and Tony has only to tinker.

"Tony," Nathan says, "after the show, drinks with Scunner?" He turns to Sandra. "Oh — you're both invited."

Sandra stares darts at Tony. He pretends not to notice. "I'm totally up for that," Tony says, "let's do it." Then, as though she's part of the equation, he adds, "Sorry, Sandra, is that alright?"

"Yeah, fine," Sandra's voice wobbles. She turns to watch the band play their final song.

"Cool," Nathan says, "see you backstage." Tony adjusts equalizers for the chorus, which sounds no better for his help. He reads the levels while Sandra sulks. After the set he pats her shoulder and heads backstage.

Tony thinks waiting to go on is the hardest part. He wants to vomit. Nathan's foot taps a frantic beat on the wood floor. Leanne and Darren share a corroded mirror, their eyes jacked open wide. Leanne checks her lashes. Darren rubs rubber cement into his hair, molds it into spikes.

They plug in; the lights come up. Tony adjusts the hi-hat. Nathan nods at Tony to start once Leanne, the real leader, counts them in, "One-two-three-four." Tony lays down a six-chord progression. The crowd roars. They know the first song, Silicone's next best thing to a hit.

After it, Tony looks to Leanne for a sign. If she's happy, he is. It's the way about her that's hooked into him more than anything physical, her bang-on arrangements, her flair. Hers is the opinion that matters.

Darren plays as asked in a band of too many chiefs. He's finally broken his habit of improvising run-on solos. He'd forget which song he was in mid-solo or start his own half-speed bluesy variation of the melody. Darren called him Lazy Fingers. Leanne had other words. "You sound like a sloth on tranquilizers." Then that would be it. They'd pelt him with cans and they were a band again. Nathan and Darren come to practices unwashed and stinking of last night's piss up. Tony reels as Leanne spurns them within an inch of their lives. He doesn't know how she does it, sorting them out without scaring them off. They don't argue, because she's right.

Tony met Leanne at a high school Battle of the Bands. Her long wide-body bass dwarfed her slight teen frame. He thought she'd topple from leaning into the mike. A performance-ready musician her age was rare. If she was airlifted to Wembly to back U2, she'd have been convincing. As a fellow songwriter, Tony knew it was her band he watched that night at school. It was Leanne who put together the set-lists and found the musicians.

He secretly fears that one day she'll walk, like Diana Ross from The Supremes. He'd be counted a hanger-on in the lead-up to her solo career, before she shed the dead weight and hit her artistic stride. Sometimes in practice, when she looks over, he thinks she's looking past him to the next stage, like he's one more hurdle to bound. She's why he stays in the band. Nathan pretends to lead. Leanne lets him shoot off his mouth then has the last word.

Tony wants to take her to bed, but they're too alike. Won't music always take precedence for her? And what about Sandra? Dare he trade his biggest fan in for another artist?

Under white light Leanne thrums a simple, definitive bass-line, a Radiohead riff. Sandra's brother sits by the wall. *Jake*. He didn't wish Leanne luck before the show. The thought distracts her on stage. She searches his eyes to check her status. Another almost boyfriend. Before Jake she had early nights. Why does she risk hard-won success for his attention? Mornings used to be sacred to her. She'd wake up excited to write, like a child getting up early to watch cartoons. With Jake she stays out, lines up in winter with other frozen women at after hours clubs. Jake prefers her in a crowd to having her alone. She follows where he leads, watches his grey eyes for approval, tries to anticipate what intrigues him, so she can be that for him. She likes his look, sure enough, cheekbones to boots.

It's a first for her, trading good looks for substance. Truth as beauty. Can it be helped? Leanne thinks. She's an artist, after all. When he feels like it, they sleep together. She's decided it's okay to be on standby if she gets to bed him, the earthly reward for the spiritual work of songwriting. She's decided that all along her songs have been about finding and losing someone like Jake.

Her baseline knits Nathan's vocals and Darren's licks into Tony's steady backbeat. Through the glare of stage lights she watches Jake eye a hardbody blond serving drinks at the next table. Sandra, sitting next to him, makes a thunderous show of applause between songs that reminds Tony of a fawning mother. He pretends not to see her.

Tony drums the coda of the fan favourite. All eyes track his arms. Sandra gets shifty. It's not because of the attention he gets, but his bond with the craft. What matters to Tony happens in the studio, away from her. Sandra wants to call herself a painter, but her work is half-assed and mediocre. So she builds sets for the Hard Times Theatre. When she took the job, Tony warned, "It'll stunt your craft." She suspects he sees in her a watered down person, afraid of her gift. She could help him – financially, anyway – until he makes it or decides to do something else. Her plans could wait, if she had any. Would it be such a sacrifice?

By the third song the buzz is back. Leanne sings with Nathan, shudders at the silent r's of his fake English accent. She tilts her bass at the amp on stage like in rehearsal. His timing's bang-on. The band's taken command, calmed down from the fright-fed rush of the opening song.

Beats last night at The Cameron. The crowd's factious attitude spoiled the performance. Silicone were discordant and noisy and never gelled. Some crowds are shark-infested. No amount of talent can curb the malicious jeers, like dogs goaded into battle. Elbows flail and guests are ejected. Nathan feeds off the rage. Darren pretends to, calls it "edgy." Tony hides behind the drum kit. Leanne wants to get offstage and reassess what she's done with her life.

They play the Queen West circuit to get their name out, promising each other it's only temporary. Three years ago they would've played for nothing. Fifty bucks apiece to do what they loved seemed like icing, until that was all they could fetch, with no pay grid rise to look forward to. "It takes fifty to rent the van for our gear," Tony pleaded to club management. Silicone was still unknown. Audiences bought in once the show got going. Before this year the band had no following. They manned the doors at their own shows, waved to passersby to lure them inside: drunk college students and underagers with nowhere else to go. They planted friends in the audience to generate buzz.

It wasn't the scene Tony envisioned, the 'happenings' in the Yorkville teahouses of the 60's. A picture of a young Joni Mitchell still hangs above his bed. He imagines her strumming an acoustic and singing in a narrow Victorian rowhouse, BP Nichol reading poetry a few doors down, Neil Young boarding in an empty room upstairs writing songs.

Tony collects vinyl records of his folk heroes: Joan Baez, Pete Seeger, Bob Dylan. One end of the room is a wall of LP's stacked in milk crates. The album covers fold open to collages of medieval pastures and space age contraptions, scenes of counter-culture 60's America. Inside the cardboard sheaths are in-sleeves printed with lyrics and liner notes. Tony prefers the heft of thirty-three-and-a-third to CD's and their flimsy inserts. He plays them on a turntable he suspended from the ceiling to prevent skips.

Nathan bristles at the retro posters and décor in Tony's room. "You're out of step," he says. "How does any of this relate to us? There's nothing folksy about Silicone. We're all short hair and gadgets. We're the guys who destroy the planet and colonize the moon." He's right about the image, Tony thinks, not the music. Silicone's songs, even the ones Nathan co-writes, impart old truths:

Will she wander, will she wait for me?

Wallet's empty, nothing guaranteed

Said she wants a cottage

In Muskoka and a boat

I just make the rent and try to keep the show afloat

They write songs of how low you can go, dirges gussied up in sunglasses and thin ties. Leanne harkens back to the beatniks and Cool Jazz for inspiration. Between sets she has the sound man play the wandering horn of Miles Davis and songs of loss and longing: Sarah Vaughn, Billy Holiday, Ella. She wishes there was a wider audience for slow lowdown songs. Sometimes she feels like she belongs in another era. Silicone's tinny sound is void of soulful sentiment — and so white. It's not her doing.

Leanne remembers the day Silicone committed to making a record. There would be setbacks later on, but it was Tony's rallying speech that April Tuesday practice that set the band's course. They were working on "Out of

Sorts," a reflective song in minor, when Tony interrupted Darren's playing, "It's more real to write what we care about than to sound like other acts. In some garage or basement, the next great group is doing their own thing. This sounds too typical." A music scene had emerged from their generation. Bands like The Arcade Fire and Broken Social Scene made it big being their uncommon selves. Musicians discarded old approaches, experimented, ignored advice. Bands controlled all sides of the business, production to marketing, CD cover art to homepage design, even after the big labels picked them up. The trend was well established. "Doesn't that make us bandwagoners," Darren said, "latecomers to a saturated market?"

"Not if we're really unique," Tony said. "There will always be haters. The music isn't for them. We can't let this artistic explosion pass without making our contribution. We're the ages of the Beatles in Hamburg on the eve of stardom."

Nathan and Darren arrived at the next practice clear-eyed and on time. The session was their most productive ever. Nathan, Leanne, and Tony shared song ideas, and the band played with new force. After practice, they went to The Yard for a pint and sat around their favourite table by the window. Other bands came in and played – Woebegone, Hegetarian, Jet Fuel – musicians their age trying to get a following. When the last band finished and the lights went up, Nathan said, "How do you think we stack up?"

Tony said, "I don't think any of those bands can touch us."

Leanne agreed, and Nathan and Darren gave Tony their full attention. "We have to get our songs to the masses," Tony said. "Music can be had cheap off the net. People only download songs they like. Every track has to count. Whole albums, without the backing of a label, are a hard sell. The safe money is in playing live. Records have become ads to sell shows."

Silicone spent that spring of their third year together building a set list. They created a fanpage with samples of their songs, self-published a CD to sell at shows. There were limits to what small acts could do. Unless they hired vans country-wide to deliver their CD's and persuaded record store chains to carry them, making records was still best left to the labels.

They sent a clean, two-song demo of their catchiest work to labels. Any record deal was a step. They lived in a state of readiness, as if by blinking they'd miss their big break. They needed a following — thousands of webpage hits and packed houses at their shows — to win a big contract. It meant ceaseless writing and teaming up with other acts to get their name out. Tony and Leanne worked part-time jobs under the table to look groomed. Nathan and Darren collected welfare. The trick was to look like they were successful and never seem desperate. They were selling a dream, hoping no one guessed that's all it was.

After rehearsal, stuffing homemade CD's in envelopes to send to record labels, Leanne, Tony, Nathan, and Darren exchanged vows. "Good music finds an audience," Tony said. "Songwriting comes first."

"And if anyone's not fully committed," Leanne said, "if you'd rather smoke pot and sleep through practices, fess up so we can find dedicated musicians." She felt like a nag. Everyone knew she was referring to Nathan and Darren. She'd found them again curled on a couch at the back of the club toking up. She was done feeling like a mom. The pot didn't phase her. She partook herself when she felt stale and sought inspiration. It was their tendency to get stuck in a holding pattern that sickened her. If she didn't track Nathan and Darren, they'd stay in a catatonic orbit, lounging in bars, eating strangers' leftovers, turning into reptiles.

The role of drugs in the band was carefully hidden from Leanne. If the male contingent had money, Jake produced the satchel of white powder he carried for a chance sell. Tony didn't smoke pot, but if the boys converged of a night flush with cash, he'd chip in for coke. They rarely had money. Tony liked his record collection too much to choke off its funding. Nathan would forgo health and possessions for a good time. He'd beaten a heroin addiction before joining the band, but lapsed since, missing two straight practices after a binge. Darren covered for him, said it was flu. He'd introduced Nathan to Tony and Leanne. They were childhood friends. When Nathan came to practice in dark glasses and long sleeves, ten pounds lighter looking ten years older, Leanne took note.

On the way from the practice, rummaging for a pick in Nathan's guitar case, Tony saw an injection kit resembling a grooming kit. He said nothing until Leanne left. On the way home he grabbed Nathan's lapels and threw him against a brick warehouse. Nathan's guitar case tumbled down the boulevard. "What're you doin'?" Darren said.

"Why don't you tell me?"

"I'm sick," Darren said.

"Sick of poking holes in your arm, you fuckin' junky?" Tony said. "I'm telling the others. You don't deserve us."

"Don't tell Leanne. I'm sorry. It's my first relapse. I spent the morning heaving into a toilet because I wouldn't go to practice high."

"Give me the rest of the stuff," Tony said.

"There is no more, man. For real, that's it."

"Give me the stuff or you're outta the band."

"You don't believe me? I wouldn't lie to you."

"You're a lying junky. Open your case and give me that kit."

"What kit are you talkin' about?" Tony crouched over the case. He reached inside and pulled out a paperback-sized black case, unzipped it and dumped the contents: pluckers, a nail file, beard scissors, and a mirror.

That was last year. After the relapse the hard drugs stopped. Silicone had momentum. A detour would spoil the big break they expected any day. Late nights had caught up with Darren and Nathan. They weren't experimenting youth who could bounce back from a binge. Years of bad diet — processed noodles and bulk snacks, cheap fixes from Kensington discount grocers — had ravaged their constitutions. Their used clothes, a bargain at point of purchase, were threadbare and molting cotton. They'd plundered the formalwear kept for special occasions and had nothing to dress up in. All had crimped in the humidity. Road salt eaten pant-legs hung ragged above their ankles.

Leanne was insulated from poverty. Waitressing tips and weekly bank deposits from Mom and Dad had furnished a snappy wardrobe. Tony made do on minimum wage. His living situation had become intolerable when, getting out of bed, he crushed his head through drywall of the low-slung ceiling of his attic apartment.

Leanne scarfed down leftovers on the way to nighttime rehearsal, beat from songwriting, serving drinks all day, and following Jake to clubs the night before. When she got off the streetcar the lights from her four-story walk-up were a hazy glow. Her head throbbed; her eyes were bloodshot slits. She fumbled for keys, finding them finally in the lining of her coat. Once inside, she dropped her bass onto the thin carpet. She looked out the dormer window at the same drunk douchebags that passed in the street last night. She put on a live Sarah Vaughan album and laid diagonally across her bed. The short mattress caused her feet to dangle off the edge. She smoked the hydroponic weed her neighbour had given her and let the music wipe her thoughts clean.

The music scene — hers anyway — was days like these. Such an expenditure for a drop of euphoria. She was too tired to masturbate. Last night's pursuit of Jake was a waste of time. She couldn't give high maintenance boys a thought at this crucial stage of her career, yet she wanted to feel his skin against her legs and chest in the half-light, feel the giddy soreness between her legs. The next day at work she stared out the window replaying the night.

2

Most of the band's family members — in their darkest hours, the band mates themselves — expect Silicone to fail, the logical outcome of missed job opportunities and abandoned degrees. Friends had entered professions, surpassing them financially, climbing to positions of influence. Silicone work in low paid service jobs: used record store clerk, waitress, window cleaner, dishwasher. Each of them could've run their workplaces. Success would've been quantifiable.

Leanne's the one most drawn to nine to five. She has a recurrent dream, ironing a white blouse in the living room of a wartime apartment, part of a uniform she wears to a job in a long, wall-less office. She's an organizer, of what doesn't matter, because the company's zombie administration treats its stock — whether chickens corralled for mass food production, slaves interned for labour, or donations registered for overseas charities — with identical detachment. She can't decide if the scene, which doesn't strike her as far-fetched, is a wish-fulfillment or anxiety dream. The dispassionate job has its appeal.

She thinks of Dad opening the tuition refund in the mail. He'd wanted her to attend teacher's college after art school, as though everything she'd done the previous four years had been a phase she'd outgrow. She applied to the Faculty of Education because he'd asked her to. The application had put him off her tracks for a while. She played the dutiful student through her acceptance of the offer to the deadline for a refund, when she turned up at the registrar's office, unloaded her I.D. on the pimply clerk and dropped out. She could've been in a placement now, singing nursery rhymes with JK's, wielding a pointer in sexless overalls.

Her mom and sister, whose lives parallel each other — part-time jobs as assistants, secure homes in executive enclaves, husbands on sure career paths — roll their eyes, repeating the refrain over interminable cups of tea: "What's Leanne thinking with this music caper?"

One of Leanne's certainties is her musical talent, another is her trustworthiness. People expect her to take charge. She could find gainful work in another field. Success, as Mom and Sis understood it, would come easily. The gains would be short-lived. Leanne's an artist.

Tony watches for awkward gestures at practice: Leanne's bangs stuck in her mouth, her skirt riding up her thighs when she dances. He enjoys the cover ups, her adjustments of bra strap and tights. She has that rare combo of tiny waste and big breasts found in women with implants or cartoon porn from Japan. Tony wakes from his gaze to her insistence: "Switch the last three chords to minor for the coda. A touch of sadness gives staying power, makes it less disposable." Once more she surprises him. He wants to get her take on art, love, the good life; but their conversation ends with the practice, as if taking it further breaks band rules.

As Silicone's profile rises, so does public scrutiny. They're local celebs. Queen Street West is a stage. Leanne daren't venture to the laundrette in her sweats. After her careful handling of P.R. on the fanpage, she asks the band, "Will our songs hold up in ten years?" She needs public approval. Sometimes the audience has no interest in original work. They want 70's rock anthems, sing-along karaoke. At their post-show debrief, Tony says, "The audience was wasted. We could've squealed and drawn applause. They're insipid. We should've played covers. That's what they like about us, that we sound like other bands."

"It happens unconsciously," Leanne says. "We write what we think is good and sound like our favourite bands. It won't hurt our popularity. Casting a wide net means we'll catch our share of ne'er-do-wells."

"And we do," Tony says.

"It's convenient, if we fizzle out, to say we weren't famous because of our integrity, as if good songwriting and success are incompatible."

"I want commercial success," Tony says.

Normally Leanne dismisses his show post-mortems as beer-induced blather. Not this time. "It's a lie to pretend we don't think about doing something else." Leanne says. "Don't you have a Plan B if the band thing doesn't work out, like a job?"

"Not really," Nathan says.

"Not I," Darren says.

"There are jobs we could do besides music," Tony says. "If we succeed we won't have to worry about them." Tony's use of 'we' stings Leanne. They're not all of one mind.

"I can't do anything else," Nathan says.

"I don't want anything else," Darren says.

"You two won't dissent in front of Tony," Leanne says. She knows they'd jump ship for a band that gave them more solos and partied harder.

Leanne checks her phone for texts. Is she withdrawing? If Silicone doesn't work out, Tony thinks it'll be her doing.

The crowd sweeps forward in unison. Guests climb the stage and dive onto outstretched arms. Bouncers book-end the stage, leery of the display. Nathan catches Leanne winking at a fan. Finally, she's happy. By the third song they're lost in performance. When Leanne's a downer and Tony talks about the future, Nathan cites times like these to bring them back. "What's so wrong with right now?" he asks. The money, of course.

Between songs Leanne taps Nathan. "Did you see him leave?" she says.

"Who, Jake?" The mid-performance pause is rare. They only break for technical problems: faulty wiring, a blown amp.

"C'mon," Leanne says, "the A & R guy, the guy who signs bands to record deals?"

"He left already? I'd forgotten he was here," Nathan says. Darren hangs up his guitar and Tony sprints out from behind the drums to join the scrum.

"I saw him leave," Darren says. "I thought he stepped out to take a call on his cell, but he didn't come back."

"That could mean anything," Tony says. They finish the set beaten.

There's no encore. Neither the venue nor their stature allow it. They're a small Indie band, assigned a slot to fill. The owner won't indulge them another minute. Lights go up before Nathan can say goodnight. The crowd streams out. Presumptuous to think they could've stretched it like headliners. They have friends who get away with drawn out Jaggeresque stage-struts, bands with albums behind them.

Jake hides most of the show on the far side of the circular bar, charming the blond shooter girl. It's the first time Leanne doesn't look for him after a show. She wants to discuss the A & R guy, knows Jake doesn't care. He steps into view with the shooter girl, downs syrupy shots whose names leave no room for innuendo: Sex-on-the-Beach, Orgasm, Slippery Nipple. Leanne turns and walks away. Music, she's relieved to find, means more to her than a selfish boy, even a hot one like Jake.

Sandra waits after the show in case Tony wants to take her home. Leanne goes to her table. "Let me guess, Tony wants to hang around a lousy bar with Nathan and that bit of Celtic tripe, Scunner?"

"Good call." Sandra says.

"Isn't he sick of the music crowd?" Leanne says.

"It's four on one if I try to pry him away," Sandra says.

"I'm sure he wants you," Leanne lies. "He's riding the wave of adulation." Leanne doesn't see Tony approach from behind. When he taps her shoulder, she blushes. "How long have you been here?" she says.

"Just got here," he says.

"Fine of you to grace us," Sandra says. "How long will you be?"

"Can't say. Another hour, longer if Scunner want to talk touring. I may not get 'round tonight. I want to 'ride the wave of adulation.'" He sees Nathan in the entrance, gesturing for them to leave. "I'll call you tomorrow."

Tony waits for Sandra's consent. Though technically she's invited, both know it wouldn't work. His friends would talk past her, in code.

Leanne leans into Sandra, whispers, "Tony's the guy you met three years ago. You didn't change him then; you won't now."

"What about Jake? Is he done with Slutoya over there?" Sandra says.

"He can have her."

"Good for you," Sandra says. "I'll call you." Leanne collects her gear on stage.

Tony reaches for the expected hug, Sandra's consent for him to leave. She's accepted this arrangement after shows — until now. "Don't wave me off like a tag-along baby sister."

"Excuse me?" Tony says.

"You heard me. Every show I wait for you to finish your *business*."

"I haven't kept you from anything. Why put this on me now?"

"Toss me aside. Your adoring fan will wait. Your friends think I'm beneath them. I can't stoop any lower. Nathan and Darren tolerate me. And Leanne — what is she to you? I'm not here to make your muse jealous. And I'm not your groupie."

Sandra's digs had always been co-conspiratorial. Tony was in on the joke. They were flesh wounds rather than death blows. Her one-way barrage lasts until closing time. He should've quit Sandra that night, walked away when she came to the The Yard the next day. he takes her punishment each time he runs into her, until, like an emptied oil drum, shaken and tilted until the last drop drips out, she's said her peace.

They do one more show that week. Leanne watches the stage before they go on. Tony drums the ground. He looks orphaned. Nathan says, "Sandra sucked the life out of you."

"So she's flawed," Tony says. "She's had me to put up with."

"You're weren't married. Don't feel so committed," Nathan says.

"Commitments keep you from drifting."

Nathan leans forward, "That'd be fine if she was your creative or intellectual equal. You can't handle mediocrity. Imagine waking to it every morning. What's the payoff: good housekeeping, flattery? How needy are you?"

"You don't know what we had."

The show is forgettable. The twelve-song set that took them four years to perfect – their best work, a cover or two thrown in for safety – feels tired. They might not reach these writing heights again. None of them expects to climb higher.

Each subsequent performance, rearranged or supplemented with new material, is formulaic. Leanne counts down the set list like days before a holiday. Winning over an audience seems like the echo of a past glory, when they could play all night and do it again the next day.

In this funk the record deal arrives. The A & R guy who'd skipped out of their show to talk on his cell phone makes a highly conditional offer: one album with national distribution and an eight city tour, including gas vouchers and a two month lease on a motor home. Silicone retains a lawyer. Under his misguidance, they sign over the international rights to all their future records.

Grateful for the lifeline, they've never felt less committed to the band.

The studio is cutting edge. They're assigned producer Todd Michaels, a former 80's singer-songwriter whose commercial success includes sentimental gems like "Nobody Loves Me" and now writes songs for other artists between production stints.

Todd just wants the record done, prefers splicing together bits of recordings to waiting for one good continuous take. In session he talks over Tony and Nathan, ignores their questions, pretends to adjust mixers. He pays Leanne more heed, but his motives are dubious. None of Silicone likes his work, but they sign off on it, sick of his warnings about the cost of studio time. Nathan challenges Todd's insertion of an instrumental middle eight, "I don't like the horns. It's not our sound."

"Horns are huge. Trust me on this one," Todd says.

"It's too 80's. I don't like it," Nathan says.

"What the fuck's wrong with that? Great music came out of the 80's."

"He doesn't think it works in this song is all," Tony says. "I agree with Nathan."

"You're saying you know better than me? I have twenty-eight years in the biz. Who the fuck are you?"

It's too late. The record's been hijacked. Three of the ten songs remain somewhat intact. Of these three, one gets college radio play ahead of the CD release.

The band demands and wins creative license over the CD cover, a black and white band photo taken on high speed film so Darren and Leanne's hands trail streaks over the guitar rosettes. Wise to the risks of overproduction, they keep the cover simple, same for the album name: "Silicone." "Self-titling is an old trick," Tony says. "It lets fans define the band for themselves."

The record's out in October. By December two songs get mainstream radio play — in Canada. Astrofix gets forty thousand downloads by Christmas. Album sales are slower. The first cheques arrive in February, a total of nine thousand dollars to be divvied between band members, thirty percent for each songwriter, ten percent for Darren, who's relegated by contract to the role of 'session musician.'

The money has to carry them through six weeks on the road. Leanne's manager says her job won't wait for her. Giving up on winning his boss's support, Tony quits the CD store.

They work their way east to west, starting in a stone tavern in Halifax by the Citadel clock. A fiery Scotts-Irish audience dances on tables, spills out of doors.

The next morning Leanne and Tony walk the rocky coastline past the city limits. Leanne summered here as a child. She wants to drink in what's on offer, to sea kayak on the Brador Lakes, hike through villages with Gaelic names. Playing music is a chore. She'd rather explore rugged wharfs in the cool wind with Tony.

The band plays a Bar Mitzvah hall in Montreal. The laminate paneled walls and intimate room are a throwback to early shows. A core of long-time fans sings along. That Silicone has a following outside Toronto who remember the lyrics is a mark of their reach. After the show, on a balcony overlooking the hall, Tony says, "They followed *us* here and came out to see *us* headline."

Leanne and Tony did it as kids: cut lawns, sold Popsicles from rickshaws to earn money for concert tickets, told their parents they were at a friend's, instead waited in the cold for a bus to the show, browsed used record stores for that hot new band that no one at school had heard of.

Devotees wait after the show to meet them. That their music makes people feel understood brings Leanne back to her teen obsessions, the delusion that poetry drips eternal from singers' mouths and real people don't exist behind their art. Bands come down from the firmament, incarnating for our betterment.

The next afternoon fans who'd huddled at the stage show the band around Montreal hotspots: vintage clothing stores in the Plateau, Latin Quarter pubs, Mount Royal lookouts with views to Old Montreal. Leanne plays the star she's supposed to be. At dinner she whispers to Tony, "This is painful." They duck out the back door of the restaurant to walk the riverbank in Lachine. Nathan and Darren's entourage crash a booze can on Rue St. Laurent.

Three nights in Montreal, a show and overnight in Ottawa, two shows over three days in Toronto, followed by a two-day drive to Winnipeg. They drive non-stop between cities, take turns at the wheel. All they do is drive and perform, too tired for much else.

The last morning in Montreal, Tony and Leanne breakfast early at the Jean Talon market, combing bakeries for fresh bread in a crowd of early risers. Undeterred by a March deep freeze, they sit and watch vendors load their stalls: mangoes, star fruit, guava, papaya. Like Nova Scotia's South Shore, the edge of Little Italy is a place where contentment seems possible. They hate to leave. Tony wants more of this, getting excited buying peppers for the meal they'd take all afternoon to prepare. The little things. He doesn't announce his intentions by a grand gesture, flowers or a slow kiss. He carries her bags and rubs her whitened, cold hands. She kisses his cheek. He brings her coffee. When he stands behind her and crosses his wrists around her waist, she's been expecting him.

In Winnipeg the chill is arctic, their impressions of the town gleaned from the closed glass balcony of a concert hall.

Drives lengthen and towns shrink until they reach Calgary. Prairie cities — Regina has it too — loom like follies in a grass desert. Calgarians, the diligent hewers of resources, dash between buildings thrown up like film sets of Old West boomtowns. The bustle is contagious.

They drive along the Bow River and camp in the Rockies, sleep by a canyon with backpackers, hike in the morning. They stay three nights, stall as long as they can before continuing to Vancouver, the last stop of the tour. They arrive ten minutes before show time bushed, guitars out of tune, voices pitchy and gruff. The grunge jam isn't had by fans who remove to the bar. Not since they started has Leanne felt so invisible. Nathan and Tony cook up a tale of a flat tire for the club owner, but it's clear to audience and bar staff Silicone aren't prepared. The owner calls the label's Artist Development arm. Tony retells the flat tire story to Sony, knowing full well that they've blown it. Short of a miracle, a surge in sales or feature in Rolling Stone – they'll be dropped. How little Tony cares, how little any of them care.

The record deal had come too late and paid them too little. Touring ate their savings. It would've cost less to rent a van and travel Canada in the pay of their old jobs, and they wouldn't have had to perform.

After the Vancouver show, the band files out the back door of the club. Nathan points to a

Western bar on Commercial Drive. "No thanks," Tony says. "Leanne and I are taking a walk."

Nathan says, "Yeah I know, pussy first right?" Before the tour Tony would've dismissed this as harmless ribbing. He throws a right hook. Batted off balance, Nathan falls on all fours. "What's that for?" he says.

"Being a musician is all you need," Tony says. Nathan looks up from the ground, mouth brimming blood. "The band's not that important to me," Tony says.

"You mean Darren and I aren't important to you."

If Leanne wasn't in the band, Nathan would've supported her pairing with Tony. But their union smacks of favoritism. Nathan and Darren no longer trust Leanne. When band members bring ideas to practice, whose will she back? Duos used to form in a spontaneous meeting of minds lasting a practice or two. Now there are two factions: the couple and the rest. To remedy it, Tony and Leanne intentionally arrive separately to practice, sit at opposite ends of the space, downplay the songs they co-wrote, heap praise on every half-baked jingle Nathan and Darren cook up. Their motive is transparent. Nathan and Darren test its limit, rapping gangsta couplets with two-note thrash accompaniments, just to watch Leanne writhe:

Yo yo yo,
This song is dope
I tolds the Pope
'Don't preach to the choir
Cuz ize on fire.'

Leanne doesn't see the humour and leaves practice fuming. Nathan leaves his best ideas at home. Darren comes to practice stoned.

Bobby Seaton, writer of *Here* magazine's "Band News and Views," foretold Silicone's demise:

Critics use the words 'electric' and 'fresh' to describe Silicone's debut album. 'Reckless' describes the tour. Silicone squandered hard-won commercial success on a badly organized road show culminating in a shoddy Vancouver jam session. Rumour has it pairing of drummer Tony Dulce and bassist Leanne McNaughton has spawned a John and Yoko-themed rift. Their scheduled appearance on Breakfast Television was canceled last week. Concert dates at the Koolhaus are postponed indefinitely.

Front man Nathan Gerber talked about touring pressures at their last show, "You do everything together on the road. It's easy to blame the friends you count on because they're always there. That's us. We forgot why Silicone started, that magic combo of solid writing and stage presence. It came so easily when we got along." Nathan's last words say it all. Silicone aren't getting along and it's coming through in their music. If they can't channel the tension creatively, expect lineup changes. Their latest release "Escapade" bears all the markings of Tony and Leanne.

3

Tony looks across his parents' yard at the porch he played on after school; the wicker chair bleachers for skateboard jump competitions off scrap plywood ramps; the net he played Twenty-One on until he moved out, still attached to the garage. The world felt smaller then, easier to navigate.

He tries to picture Nathan dribbling on a driveway, repairing a bike, mowing the lawn. This childhood scene and Nathan don't mesh. Tony can't decide what bugs him more, the truth in Nathan's comments about Sandra and Leanne or the liberty he took in making them.

When Darren and Nathan sabotage practice, Leanne and Tony don't try to stop them. Collaboration is beside the point, since no one is writing music anymore. Small tasks — attaching cords, tuning a guitar — sting under the scornful glares of the other faction. In rehearsal, songs that had taken years to perfect sound amateurish.

All spring Silicone lurch between reunion and retrenchment of the two camps. In a last gasp of band spirit, Leanne asks the label to spring for jackets with the band logo, a mountain-shaped breast with a snow-covered nipple, embossed on the back. What they get are purple satin bomber jackets, the top halves of roller derby get-ups. Nathan won't wear his in public. Darren chucks his in the dumpster behind the rehearsal space.

On Labour Day they play The Horseshoe Tavern, their first show in five months. Leanne won't look at Nathan and Darren. The factions speak only on matters of business. Before the show, Bobby Seaton sits down with Tony, who tries to steer him off rumours of discord: "Touring was a wild ride. We're still coming down. When we do, we'll pick up where we left off, best of mates, like nothing happened." Tony lies out of caution. Contractual obligations might keep the band together for some time.

After the show, a familiar outline cuts through the stage lights. *Sandra.* Tony waits for her to hit or publicly defame him, but she crosses the floor to Leanne, bypassing him without a look in his direction. "I expected as much from Tony," Sandra says, "but really, my boyfriend and my best friend?"

"This," Leanne steadies herself, "doesn't touch our friendship. We fell into it. I don't know how it happened. I didn't orchestrate it."

"I needed to talk. The split was hard." Sandra's shoulders droop. "I'm at that age."

"What do you mean?" Leanne says.

"The age of having a plan — career, marriage, real stuff."

Leanne reaches out her hand. Sandra recoils. "You think this was my plan? Giving up on a project I spent a chunk of my life on?" Leanne says. "I make the band unworkable."

"At least you have someone to share your disappointments," Sandra says, shoulder pointed at Leanne.

"Isn't that what we're doing, sharing disappointments?" Leanne says.

"Don't pretend to understand. When you leave here, Tony will fuck your worries away in his crawlspace. You'll share a laugh at the byoch who stalked you at the show."

"You think I'm so heartless?" Leanne says. "*You* bed Tony. He's right there. I won't stop you."

Sandra covers her mouth with her hand. "I'm not here for him. Everyone's moved on but me." She walks away.

Leanne sits at Tony's drum kit, taps the symbols. "I should go home alone," Leanne says, knowing she won't follow through. "I can't relate to the songs I wrote. What happened to us these past four years? I don't know my bandmates."

"We barely knew ourselves. We were kids striving to be something," Tony says. Their hit, Astrofix, is playing in the background. "What were we really after? Attention? Respect? I've no idea." He rubs his eyes, leans on his knees. "Is Sandra alright?"

"I've had the tour and you. She's on her own. I can touch the hearts of fans. I can't keep my best friend."

"You give people your music."

"Most of my music was made with one band. None of us chose to leave the band and we're not together."

"Because none of us are fighting to keep the band alive," Tony says.

———————

Tony listens to Silicone's demo, digs out old promo posters rescued from lamp-posts and bathroom mirrors: black and white montages of the band with other acts: Hijinks, Ripple, Thin Edge of the Wedge, Scunner. In every pic, Leanne's eyes pierce the viewer. Her bandmates' expressions are foggy. At least Nathan looks like a rock star. Tony invited him into the band because Nathan makes up the rules as he goes — or appears to. It isn't all show. He has the face of a man who's pulled too many all-nighters, a slave to his art with a loose grip on basic self-care and hygiene. Yet he has more fun in the band than Tony and Leanne.

Their first practices were in Tony's parents' garage. Kids from the nearby public housing played basketball on Tony's six-car driveway while skate punk blared from an amplifier. Neighbours expected him to stay here, presiding over local disaffected youth like a camp counselor. When he moved out, Tony couldn't stop directing. This feeling that he was a chief never left him. Leanne felt a similar calling. Both were slightly embarrassed by the band, this limb they'd climbed out on.

After the show, Leanne says, "I'm gonna

go, guys. I have to grab my gear from The Horseshoe first thing in the morning. I need sleep." She picks up her equipment that night in a taxi with Tony, doesn't care if she's caught in the lie. The band don't know that's the last show they'll play together.

No one calls a practice that week or the next. Tony sleeps in, roots through his record collection for nostalgia. Carol King. When he taps along to the music, his fingers cramp up. How soon, untended, virtuosity is lost. In high school a skate-boarding injury had forced him onto crutches until his leg muscles atrophied. On his second try catching air off a half-pipe, he'd swung in too far from the rim and landed on one knee. A loud pop then screams in the fulcrum of the ramp. Three years of conditioning lost. He'd been in the best shape of his life.

Off school for five weeks, Tony missed track and field try-outs and was lucky to graduate with his peers. The accident upended university plans. With upper body intact, Tony drummed in the empty house. In the way that deprivation of one sense heightens others, Tony's arms quickened. He conquered the signature solos of Bonham, Peart, Rich. While friends visited campuses and chose courses, he searched music store message boards for drummer want-ads. Nathan's stuck out:

If you don't miss a beat, beat your way past my door. Vocalist/rhythm guitarist looking for drummer to steal shows.

Nathan seemed like someone cool to hang out with.

When the Carol King record ends Tony answers old emails. He watches a screensaver of a U.F.O. ricochet off the sides of the monitor. He used to spend this hour updating the band fanpage. He'd snack at his desktop, writing blogs to try to make the band sound interesting. "I spend more time advertising my life than living it," he'd complained in rehearsal.

"That's self-promotion," Leanne had said, "making much of little. That's how art's sold now."

"And if I don't want to? There's no freedom in it."

"No choice. Welcome to 24-hour surveillance," Nathan said. "Big brother's a 14 year-old with a cell phone, your every move recordable and uploadable to immortal cyberspace. You can run but you can't hide. If you're not online, you don't exist."

After work Tony would sit on the futon making words fit melodies. Weeks went into writing one verse that the band couldn't fault. Three tracks on the record were written this way. He thought if he ever had the time, he'd read industry mags, a Melody Maker or Rolling Stone; or search for the guitar tabs of his favourite songs, so he could strum along like he did in high school.

Now that he has more time, he loafs around like an old man looking back on a misspent life, slipping into reveries that slide into naps. He recounts his dreams in vivid detail when he's awake, thinking he's still in the tour van on the way to a show. In one dream the van has crashed. He finds the lifeless band members scattered along the otherwise barren road. He prepares the eulogy, selects tombstones and caskets. He misses the viewing because he's too busy making funeral arrangements.

It's clear that he never had a Plan B in case the music fell through. He waits for Leanne to arrange another rehearsal. When the call doesn't come, an abyss takes the place of the music career he'd envisioned.

Tony keeps checking the fan page. He returns the LP's to the milk crate, his final pre-rehearsal act, but there's no rehearsal.

The label had fitted them out for the tour: p.a's, effects peddles, guitar stands. Who gets what? As a non-writer, Darren was paid like a session musician. He'll leave Silicone a beggar. After the wrangling over creative property, Tony wonders whether Nathan and Darren will ever want anything to do with him.

4

Leanne lies in bed watching the ceiling stipple. She won't bring an idea to practice. The lease on the rehearsal space is up. She falls asleep then wakes bolt upright, reviews her dream to get the sequence straight. She can't form a whole, but a part of it is clear: She's gliding alone into infinite space, cast from the ship by its on-board computer. She's Frank in *2001: A Space Odyssey*.

She'll go for coffee — yes, a coffee, maybe chat with the server. She hasn't read in months. She could do that. She found a job in a bar on Ossington Avenue by the asylum. Her four-hour shift doesn't start until two and Tony's at the CD shack. Leanne can't fill a day with puttering. The long downtime is a slow death.

She could go to school. She'd be on her own with fees after the teacher's college fiasco. She checks the message board at the Royal Conservatory for work as bass instructor. The

Program Director lays it out for her, "Most bass players are self-taught, usually guitarists picking up a second or third instrument. You may want to rethink teaching music."

Playing guitar as a teen, Leanne felt like a misfit. She misses that time. One formative moment stands out, winning backstage passes to Attaché. The show had spurred her to reinvent herself. She couldn't pinpoint the turning point. She likes to think it was the music not the celebrity, but it was the whole grainy mess of the show: fans aching for a wider world than home: the sweet pungency of pot, alcohol, promiscuity; and at its heart, the performance itself.

Leanne met singer Liam Matthews. She knew his biography before brushing by him backstage. The mere fact of his talking to her was a thrill, and she wanted to have that kind of hold on people.

"Has fame changed your life?" Leanne asked. She struck Liam as too vulnerable to be furnished with half-truths. Her backstage access gave him the impression that she worked for a teen mag. He didn't want some tawdry phrase slapped on a fanzine with his pic at a jaunty angle. Media underreported his writing prowess, as if his songs were ghostwritten while he reveled

217

on yachts. Fans should know the artist, not the promo tool.

"It's funny," Liam said, "how little fame changes who you really are. Your image circulates. Fans project their dreams onto you. The dream is famous, not you."

"You must love the attention?"

The attention isn't for you," Liam said. "Get honest with media and you're no longer that star shrouded in mystery."

"You must love making music for a living though?" Leanne said.

"You have to bring it every show. When it works something magic ignites between audience and band. Then it ends. After touring I don't know what to do with myself. I chase drugs and loose women. You have to get back to writing. That's the come down. It's fine when the writing flows, but when you're blocked? You prime the pump with stimulants – coffee, speed, Red Bull, coke – it's a needle that won't break the skin."

"I play bass in a band," Leanne said. "It's going nowhere." Liam's doubts about music are problems she wants to have. What's the source of his power?

"You'll make it if you put in the time," Liam says. "Work through the lows. A band's a family. It's harder on your own. Think of Elvis. I used to write for my school paper. Nearly became a journalist. To stare at a screen punching keys in solitude. No thanks."

"I write poetry," Leanne said.

Liam tousled her hair. She thought, *He can take me now on the sofa if he wants.* He looked her over. They were ten years apart. It seemed to her like a generation. "I have to go. Don't waste your talent," Liam said.

Attaché is still cited by rising alt rock acts as a major influence. The band outgrew its cult status because of quality song-writing. Clever arrangements had won over the musicologists. Liam's soft features tickled the 13 year-old girl demographic.

"So you're telling me, 'Be cool, stay in school'?" she said.

"I'm saying work hard," Liam said.

Leanne thinks she's worked hard. She'd kept the high school boys at bay without resorting to the promise ring the evangelicals wore. Her single-mindedness had put her on a footing with serious musicians.

She stops at the entrance to Philosopher's Walk outside The Royal Conservatory, adjusts the strap on her guitar case, strides between the ivy-cloaked university buildings, feeling none of her teen affection for the campus. What institution prepares you for the compromises of adulthood?

She could start over, pin a "bassist available" sign on the message board at Steve's Music store like she did eight years ago. *No way.*

The Conservatory appointment was shorter than she'd expected. With time to kill before her shift, Leanne drops by Pages Bookstore, scans the magazine rack. *NME* has an exposé on Liam. Attaché are getting the retrospective treatment of other disbanded alt rock super groups: The Smiths, Stone Roses, The Cult. The article recounts Liam's stormy odyssey through North England's club circuit before his 'overnight success.' Leanne had measured her milestones against his: first band, first song, first paid gig. At age seventeen she'd set deadlines for the first record, the first tour. If planning killed the joy of playing, it now seems she didn't plan enough ahead.

Leanne arrives for her shift. Waiting to collect drinks, she overhears a man tell the bartender, "I don't know how stage actors perform the same play a thousand times." She remembers saying something similar to justify folding the band to Tony, "I couldn't repeat the writing-album-tour cycle. *Boring*." As she puts the drinks on her tray and navigates the afternoon barflies, the irony of the remark isn't lost on her. It turns out there are degrees of boredom.

She'd enjoyed aspects of Silicone, but Nathan's uniform of tatty shirts and jeans scared her. When she moved to Kensington Market in college, she'd hidden a past of European vacations and Muskoka family weekends from her housemates. She under-spent them, cut her own hair, took simplistic leftist views on social issues to blend in.

On cold days homeless men slept in the doorway of her walk-up. She shared the carved up manse with students and mental health out-patients. Shut-ins on her floor counted on Leanne to get their groceries and make small repairs.

A roommate took her to a protest over tuition hikes. Leanne's lyrics became social commentary. She brought her acoustic to the open mike at Che's Bistro weekly, until a heckler called her preachy.

In her apartment she felt like a tourist. When a hard rain drove through the flashing and flooded her room, she moved out and enrolled in design, her Plan B if music didn't pan out. Through this period, something her father had said kept crossing her mind, "You only have what you create."

A customer hands Leanne his stein. "My beer's flat."

"The keg must be empty or the pump needs priming," she says.

"Do you know how to pour a pint?"

"It took drinking the whole pint for you to figure out it's flat?"

"Excuse me?"

"Sorry, I'll get you a fresh one."

With Silicone gone, Leanne could finally branch out and work with new talent. Instead she lounges after work with Tony, having the kinds of conversations she imagines couples across the city are having. She doesn't write music that fall.

Business picks up as the dinner crowd streams in. Leanne talks to customers, doesn't see that Fred and Steve from rival band The Blowhards are waiting for her to take their order. "Sorry, what can I get you?" she says.

"I'll take your record deal," Fred says.

"It's yours," Leanne says.

"I don't get you," Steve says. "You had what we want. Now you're schlepping drinks?" He licks his lips. She's repulsed. The room's an unlikely mix of leather-clad punk hold-outs and the suits displacing them as Queen West gentrifies. "This gig's temporary," Leanne says. A Florence and the Machine song that Leanne had the sound guy play between Silicone's sets plays in the background.

"You fucked it up," Fred says. Foam gathers in the corners of his mouth. "Why don't you join The Blowhards?"

"Yeah, cuz then you can blow me really hard," Steve snorts.

"Real original, Steve. I'll get back to you on that." Leanne walks off holding her nose.

5

Leanne stays with her parents over Christmas. She hasn't slept at home since college, can't relax in the old room. She bakes puff pastries with her sister Tina, helps Dad build an ice rink for her nephew. He doesn't ask about the band, doesn't tell her he's worried. Tina and her mom behave for a while, then the probing starts. When Mom asks about the size of her apartment, Leanne says she's going home to the city.

Her friends already have set design jobs: Sandra in a private school theatre, Victoria on a film sound stage. Leanne turns down their invitations to go out, revives her portfolio, contacts well-connected former teachers. Her take-home pay is better than Tony's. A weekend's tips beat what either of them makes in salary, yet she's broke. "I can't make a life out of the bar," Leanne tells Tony. She calls in sick, fires off applications, books interviews. She launches an earnest job search, the beginning of a productive tear that could last the rest of her working life. She'll go it alone if Tony can't keep up.

Tony looks out the CD shop window at cranes overhanging concrete pilings. Steel skeletons rise higher by day over Queen Street, drawing eyes upwards. Toronto is booming. Career types he'd looked down are reaping the rewards of persistence. The boom's well on in its cycle. The upswing will pass.

Silicone's breakup — not a year old — still rankles. What if he made a final push? Parlay the first record deal into a bigger one with another label? Darren and Nathan have moved on to other bands. If he asked them, would they come back?

Tony walks into the sales centre of a condo project a block from work. It's like others downtown: live/work spaces with open tread staircases, ten foot ceilings, operable paper-thin walls — at unaffordable prices. Toronto too expensive for Torontonians. They buy anyway.

Tony lies about his income on a registration survey, fills out his email address in the requisite field, so he can be spammed for the rest of his life. An agent takes his clipboard, leads him to a room with a model of a high rise and floor plans on the walls. Tony's sequestered with other visitors so all can hear the same pitch.

He feigns interest in the projections on the wall: beautiful people on patios, boomers doing Tai Chi in Grange Park under sunny skies. He examines the plans of the unit he'd buy if he had money and chose this one from among thousands across the city.

The sales rep's shoes are polished, hair tinctured. The bare nape of his neck screams obsessive grooming. Beside him and the prospective buyers, Tony feels downmarket. He's missed a window. People his age are passing him by. His faded khakis are creased and ill-cut.

The agent finishes his pitch. They move to the model suite. Tony asks the rep whose nametag identifies him as Bill, "How'd you get this gig?"

"You mean working here?" Bill says.

"I mean real estate?"

Bill considers the question, it being awhile since anyone took an interest in his job or him. He tells Tony about the real estate course. The first Tuesday of July, Tony's in a class taught by a retired realtor.

6

The loonie climbs to parity with the U.S. dollar. Film set work in Toronto dries up. When Leanne is offered a community theatre job outside the city, she daren't decline. Her role is Set Director.

Ashfield's Centre for the Performing Arts is lavish compared to the firetrap downtown theatres. The iconic glass box is the centerpiece of Town Council's Main Street revival, an effort to ground residents' Toronto-bound flights for culture. Ashfield's charms are well-known, but its theatres hail from humble beginnings. Thousands of recent immigrants have settled in the town's more affordable north. Council is building big institutions for a big posterity. In the Centre Leanne is an organizer. She hopes someday to write scores for a musical troupe on its way up, to be an unofficial artist-in-residence.

From her office above Main Street, she watches swimmers leave the public pool, square-jawed mesomorphs in tight athletica, hair straggly and damp. She loves the vigour of the place. People here take care of themselves.

By week's end the airy Centre feels shrunken-down. All day she's on the phone to suppliers. Staff don't ask her to lunch. They fear and pity her for her trifling power over them. She can't concentrate. Why did she leave the city? Where the Featured Artist Gallery and Performing Arts Centre lobbies intersect, a docent slurps coffee on one of the loveseats. They haven't met, but Leanne overheard her talk about a documentary at the film festival. Leanne sits across from her. "Checked out any films at TIFF?"

"Did you say something?" the docent says.

Leanne's question was loud, clear, unmistakable. "Oh no." She walks outside, watches old men wipe down their yachts in the harbor, leans her elbows on the railing of the bridge, face in hands. She can't afford doubts. Being outside the length of a cigarette break feels like skiving off. The Aladdin set demands all her attention.

Since there are more realty offices than theatres, Tony follows Leanne to Ashfield. It eats him to be the one to follow. When they walk Lakeside Park Pier with hot ciders, his male pride abates somewhat. Ashfield is an artists' colony — for artists with money. Urban without the grit, theme parkish and over-programmed in its public spaces, yet not wholly given over to retirees. There are by-laws concerning lawn length and driveway design; Parks & Rec seminars on health promotion and wellness; roadside hanging gardens tended by the Ashfield Horticultural Society; hiking trails with circuit training stations and ultra-safe playgrounds.

Tony joins an established brokerage, Old Ashfield Realty. He has to move high volumes of low-end homes to stay on the team. His broker, Arthur, won't let rookies sell mansions. Janet his manager has a middling sales record. Her title brings no added compensation, yet she seizes on small distinctions between herself and her charges. "You're in over your head," she whispers to Tony.

He and Leanne rent a small flat. Even though Leanne works late most nights, they make time to walk along the lake watching sailboats trawl in and out of the harbour. All over Ashfield residents run, bike, and rollerblade on the shoulders of the one-lane roads. There are no nightclubs. The restaurants are above Tony and Leanne's price point. When a gym goes up on their street, they buy memberships.

Tony actually uses his. He goes after

showings, preferring the gym to the empty apartment.

A red-haired girl comes in while Tony's on the ski machine. She's fit, doe-eyed, younger. He's on the machine weights beside her. She cycles through a step program attached to a set of earbuds, flashing polite smiles when he goes to the rack to change weights. He's intrigued by a hand-sized sketch pad she doodles in on the step machine console. It's a game, timing his transitions between sets with her breaks. "What are you listening to?" Tony finally asks.

"Me?" She adjust the volume on her device. "The Black Keys mostly, some Arkells. Wanna hear?" She dangles the earbuds in front of him.

Tony holds them both against one ear. "My band played stuff like this," he says.

"You're in a band?"

"Used to be. Heard of Silicone?"

"Uh, yeah. I loved that first album." She sits down, hangs her towel over the bench. "Why didn't you guys put out more music?"

"Good question," Tony says.

"I'm Renata by the way." She smiles.

"Tony." He reaches forward then withdraws. "You probably don't want my sweaty hand."

"I'm just as bad." Renata's cell phone rings. "I better take this." Before he's done a set of squats, she's waving goodbye.

He thinks about her between showings, reschedules appointments to time his trips to the gym with hers.

He's lying on a bench when she brushes past. "Hey," he calls.

"I forgot how awesome Silicone was. I downloaded a few of their tunes."

"That's encouraging," Tony says. He gets up, but she's gone to the step machine. He finds her at the water bottle refill. "Is there anything to do in this town?" he says.

"What do you want to know? I *am* from here." Renata talks about ice-cream parlours and the Waterfront Fair. He listens to her talk on the phone to her mom about summer jobs. She's young. He feels too aimless to play the part of mentor, yet at work his mind wanders to her body and silk voice.

Tony enjoys colleagues' complements on

his buff new look. Real estate tests him, holding uncontroversial court with clients in the pine-scented cabin of his leased luxury sedan. He senses their distrust, a pulling away when he asks after their families, their lies told to end a conversation. He hangs onto promises they forgot making: "I'll be in touch about the place on Brookside." His take away is that they don't take him seriously. He looks too young. Tony's olive skin disguises his age. He can't turn verbal agreements into binding contracts. When he sells, Janet mocks the generosity of his purchase agreements, won't sign off on them without revision. After a late viewing, he finds her in his office reading a prospectus. "Why are you here?"

"Sorry, a client just asked about the features at Montmorency place."

"It's on the website. Stay out of my office." He can't prove Janet's poaching his clients. Anyway, Arthur wouldn't believe him. Tony's an unknown. His colleagues count on referrals and returning clients. Tony's still building a client base. He lives out of his car, skips lunch to show homes to lukewarm prospects. He's learning the psychology of sales: how to stage viewings and whittle sellers on price. A coat of paint adds unwarranted thousands to a home price. Details break deals. Eyes home in on rumpled carpet, a messy line of grouting. He takes better care of his wardrobe, shops on Boxing Day for the Ted Baker suit and Maui Jim sunglasses. "You made a choice when you moved here," Arthur had told him early on. "Look the part."

Tony shows Leanne a row house on the northern edge of town. It's small, but they want out of their rental. "You wouldn't know we earn good coin," he says. "We'll be mortgaged to the hilt."

"Wiser to own," Leanne says. Practicality scares Tony. He likes the idea of stability, yet he longs to transgress. He wants to smoke up with the teens loitering in Lakeside Park, to hang around bars and pick up a pretty woman with a voluptuous body and seduce her shamelessly.

At the gym, he makes his move. Renata has a knowing crook in her thin smile. Lust feels different from when he was younger, more predatory. "What are you up to after this?" Tony says.

"What do you mean?" Renata says.

"After your workout, can you join me for a drink?"

"I'd love to, but I have to get home. Do you have a SmackChat account?"

"I'll get one."

On the way home, a Benz stops on the bridge in front of Tony, blocking the lane. A man in a bowling shirt with a contemptuous trimmed beard gets out of his car and cleans off his windshield. Tony honks. The man mouths, "One minute." It's the presumption that irks Tony, the apparent sense of entitlement he has to impose himself. Tony wants to launch the car off the bridge with the man inside it. He rolls down his window, shouts, "What gives you the right?" The man sticks up his middle finger and speeds off. Tony fist hammers the steering wheel, honks, laughs at the implausibility of his life here.

Leanne is working late. She's on the phone fielding questions about the theatre company from suppliers: Is it a cast of over forty? Do they have budget for a dumbwaiter? She wants to delegate the search for answers to their questions. The Centre's full of A-type personalities trying to organize each other. She calls her Person Friday Angela, who struts into Leanne's office and plunks herself down on the desk. "Know up front that I'm not your servant."

"Excuse me? Who are you again?"

Leanne says.

"Angela. I don't know how you got this job. What are you, twenty-seven?"

"Twenty-six."

"That's *my* age," Angela says. "Who'd you fuck on the board? I'm curious who pressured HR."

"Thanks for the welcome, *assistant*. You can go, I have work to do." Leanne waves her off.

"Easy. I'm sure you've got the quals." Angela is fully accessorized — Thai silver bracelets, pearl necklace, 'model off duty' Row t-shirt — hardly the hungry intern Leanne expected.

"I'll only be the newbie a short while," Leanne says. It's too soon to fire people. She needs allies. She closes her door, picks up the phone, puts it down. There's no one to vent to. She sees the board chairs cut out early from the top floor for golf, backslapping and cracking conspiratorial jokes. They think she's rigid. She wishes she could relax, wishes she could join them.

Having set up a SmackChat account, Tony's pleased to find Renata waiting when he gets online. "How was your day?" he types.

Minutes pass without a response. Maybe she's chatting with someone; maybe this isn't even her account. The phone pings.

"Awful," Renata writes beside a pic of herself crinkling her nose.

Tony snaps himself with a quizzical open mouth. "What happened? Mine blew too. Nothing tragic, just dull. Paperwork, emails."

"Just overwhelmed by assignments. I'm still in school."

"Take it in. You won't be that free again." Catching himself mentoring, Tony changes course. "On another note, I think you're hot."

"You're attractive too. R u in a relationship?"

"Nothing serious. What r u up to?" Tony snaps a selfie with wry smile.

"Talking to you, lmao!"

"Ha ha," Tony writes. He doesn't expect what comes next: a pic of Renata in peach lingerie.

"You like?"

"Uh...yeah!" The next sequence: pics of her bare chested with towel draped around waist; on back in a bed, legs spread; perched naked on the edge of the kitchen counter. She's done this before. The pics are old.

"OMG!" Tony writes, faking shock. Her language after that contains more filth than he'd imagined her young mind possessed, yet a pornographer's turn of phrase comes just as easily to him.

When the sexting gets repetitive, Tony says, "We have to hook-up."

"When and where?"

"Tomorrow after the gym, my place."

Tony reschedules late-day appointments, ignores a client complaint of too few visitors at the open house. He may lose the contract if he doesn't rally interest in the property. He doesn't care.

At the gym Renata flashes her usual crooked smile. "See you out front in ten or fifteen?" he asks after the workout.

"For sure."

He waits outside, still wet after a frenzied workout. Leanne texts him. He looks up from his phone to an unsmiling Renata. "No offense, Tony.

I don't think you're my type."

"What about last night online?"

"That was different."

"I don't see how."

"You're attractive and interesting. I'm after a different kind of man."

"Really?"

"I'm sure. This happens on dates sometimes."

"I didn't know our date had started."

"Sorry."

Rereading Renata's messages in his car, Tony feels duped, deservedly so. The sum total of his social media experience is the band's fanpage. He shouldn't have yielded to her pre-packaged posts. Virtual cheating is too easy. He feels low, worse about attempting to have a real fling. He's never expressed desire so directly. He'd like to think he's become more assertive. He just feels selfish.

Tony thinks about Leanne. What about her self-interest? He followed her to Ashfield. She's the ambitious one. Yes, but she hasn't misrepresented herself. He should've known what he signed up for when he moved here.

Leanne organizes all aspects of *The Taming of The Shrew* up to opening night. The next day her head's in the next production. She doesn't use the lull in the schedule to refresh.

Suppliers take advantage of her. Reluctant to play hardball, she overpays them. Her set is too tailored to one show to be of use in another. She's relieved when the new troupe brings a stage-ready set. The board overlooks her shaky start. Her sets come in functional and on time.

After work she reheats the dinner Tony left. He's sleeping. "Guess we're not going for a walk?" She climbs into bed, her gym membership remains untouched on the side table.

When Leanne's late again the next day, Tony digs through his belongings, weighs the merits of moving out. He finds his drums in a box stowed away since the move, sets it up in the basement.

He attempts the solos of his drum heroes. Unpracticed, his fingers seize up. Without musicians to pace him, he loses time. Pain shoots through his foot when he lifts it off the pedal. He thinks about the time Silicone shut down the Rivoli. Crowd and band, for two hours of their lives, were in sync.

He misses virtuosity. Without a band to push him, performing live again seems too steep a climb. Where are Ashfield's musicians? A banker at the gym plays guitar; a client plays sax. Neither of them has been a full time musician.

Leanne finds Tony on the back deck. "You okay?"

"I'm tired," Tony says, "not sleepy or sore. It's nothing physical."

"You're tapped out?"

"Yup."

"I'm there too," Leanne says.

"We're too young to feel like this," Tony says.

"Do you feel trapped?"

"Not by you," he says too quickly. "It wouldn't matter who you were."

"Gee thanks."

"I mean it's a self problem."

"Okay."

"I haven't got worse at my job. I just don't know why I'm doing it."

"Because you're good." Leanne bites her lip, raises an eyebrow. Tony loses his train of thought, suddenly aware of her white cotton dress, suddenly aware that he wants it off. He sticks a finger in her armpit. She slinks back, pounces on him, tickles his ribs. He picks her up, lays her supine on the cedar planks.

After the euphoria, they fall asleep on the deck, her head in the crook of his arm. He starts instigating more quickies. It's stimulation he's after. He used to leave the gym on a high, brain awash in serotonin. Now he drinks espresso and Coke to simulate the effect. He keeps toned women at the gym in his sights, hoping they care that he's looking.

Tony loads his Ipod with his best estimate of what the alt-rock kids are into: Arctic Monkeys, Bloc Party, Walls of Jericho, Suicide Silence. It worked when he was fourteen trying to seem hip. He'd learned to mimic fans, to trick older musicians into thinking he was well-versed.

The brokerage is five blocks from the Centre for the Performing Arts in a homey grand

Victorian manse. Tony's office backs onto a deep yard with lilies and chestnut trees. He should like it. He doesn't. He thinks about moving back to the city to give music one more try — with Leanne if she'll bite. She's jammed once since moving to Ashfield. It stung him to hear the ground she'd lost.

The workload lightens. Only weeks ago Tony held multiple viewings on a weekday, closed deals by handshakes in living rooms, because he couldn't put the paperwork together fast enough to meet the demand. His tardy removal of lawn signs, as the latest offers stole his attention, was a sticking point with Albert. Now Tony's desk is clear. Agents have slumps, but it's as though a switch has flipped at the brokerage.

Months pass without an uptick. Sellers extend their agents' contracts or take their homes off the market. Realtors who guarantee a sale — "If I don't sell your home, I'll buy it" — declare bankruptcy. From a seller's to a buyer's market overnight. Agents arrive at work early, groomed, and alert. A hush has come over the brokerage.

On the way home, where the leafy one-lane artery becomes a three lane obstacle course of medians and turning funnels, Tony pulls onto the Toronto-bound ramp. It's rush hour. He has a vague destination in mind. Darren has moved house, didn't tell Tony where. He could go to Nathan's.

Queen Street is fully gentrified. Condos and furniture emporiums have made this once derelict stretch unrecognizable. Few of the taverns where they played are still in disrepair. Tony parks and walks to The Cameron, sits at one of the chintzy tables at the back and orders a drink. His wallet is flush with cash. Beside the server, with his combat boots and cargo pants, Tony feels like an imposter slumming it, Howard Hughes hitching a ride in *Melvin and Howard*.

Patrons enter in groups. He saw the band that's setting up years ago: Nose Job. He had a thing for the keyboard player, remembers noting that none of them had actually had a nose job. His eyes widen as Darren joins the band on stage wearing giant hoop earings, his hair in a vertical Pebbles pony tail. Darren nods at him.

After the show, Tony retreats to the bar by the entrance. He'd go backstage to compliment the band, but Darren's glib nod has set the tone. The bartender is fit and pale with thick Goth eyeliner and blue-black hair, wearing an ankh pendant and a short skirt. He used to tell Nathan and Darren, "One girl you can always talk to is the bartender. She can't leave." "Not a bad show," Tony says.

"Alright. Not much of a crowd," the bartender says. She pours whiskey into a snifter, sits on a stool, downs it. She catches Tony ogling her legs, knits her brows. Tony is getting ready to leave when Darren sits down beside him.

"S'up?" Darren says.

"You guys sounded great," Tony lies.

"Just filling in. Their lead guitarist is touring Holland. I'm actually with Shaman now. We're gunning for a spot in North by Northeast."

"Oh yeah," Tony says, "How long have you played together?"

"Two weeks, but we've got plans."

"Sounds like it," Tony says.

"What about you? Marriage treating you well? Heard you're selling used cars or something?"

"I'm not married, and it's real estate. Whatever. How's Nathan?"

"Awesome. He's in Scrotum."

"Really?" Scrotum was breaking out of the local scene around the time Silicon disbanded.

"Yeah. They just got signed to Warner U.S.A." Tony gulps. Silicone coveted a U.S. contract. Their label wanted to build Silicone's profile in Canada before pitching to its U.S. parent.

Tony and Darren go to Kensington for Vietnamese food. If both are jealous of one another, neither of them would trade places. The rift between them is too recent to drown in bowls of pho. Tony wishes it wasn't. "We have to stay in touch."

"Always, Dude," Darren says into his noodles. The two lock fists and hug, but Tony feels brushed off.

On the way to the parking garage, he recognizes Leanne's old four storey walk-up and the bistro across the street where she performed at open mike. Even the servers who come into view through the windows are the same. On the highway he's part of the closing time exodus. He carries on past the Ashfield exit, passes five more exits before pulling off at a truck stop in Hamilton. Only the gas pumps are open and has to drive downtown to find an open diner. He orders coffee. A young man sits by the window on a laptop. Two women still in servers' uniforms from another restaurant share rhubarb pie at the bar. There are the anonymous retired men who come for the slim chance of good conversation, sitting alone at tables for two. He gulps his coffee and settles the bill, drives along the lake road, passes loud drunk teens. Downtown Ashfield is vacant. When he gets home, Leanne's car is in the driveway. He'd hoped she was awake. She's not. Tony climbs into bed, nuzzles the back of her head, shuts out the night.

"No mortgage means no purchase," Tony says. He shakes the hands of the young couple, shows them the door. He's learned the art of thwarting dreams, has it down to two sentences. He could avoid confrontation by sending them to lenders with loan shark rates. The outcome would be the same.

He buys an espresso and walks to the lake. A couple is on the concrete breakwater snogging. Small sloops and cutters run their outboards, the breeze too gentle to fill sails.

He's dispatched to meet a young father, Sam, at an empty mansion whose deadbeat owner let it fall to ruin. Sam plans to restore it on weekends. The pool's liner has peeled. Its concrete coping has crumbled, exposing rebar. A new owner could add tens of thousands to the price through minor renoes.

Sam dives into projects without grasping the work involved. When he catches on he's too far along to quit. This time Sam's done the calculations. An outhouse would cost in this lakeside location. He put his antique collection on Ebay to raise the down payment.

Tony shows him the home five times that summer. Sam maps it mentally. Tony indulges Sam's dream because he's secretly pulling for him, has seen his sort before, the visionary of the yard after it's leveled and re-sodded, the new French balcony where the pediment is sagging. Why didn't he check Sam's credit score? Tony invites him to the brokerage to tell him face to face that the house is out of reach. He owes him that.

A purge is underway in real estate. Forced to unload homes at fire sale prices are the company transfers, the newly redundant and downsized. Few realtors believed the condition that buoyed them for so long could change: rising home prices.

In the downturn work at the Centre picks

up. People find money in their tightened budgets for more live theatre. Leanne adds a matinée on weekdays, starts work early to prep for it. Her office has a loveseat. When her blood sugar drops, she naps.

Tony has more energy than he knows what to do with. He lingers at the gym. There's no Renata whose attentions he commands. The women who come in have commitments and self-control. After weights, he works his knuckles raw on the punching bags. When the weather agrees, he walks.

He's on a disused road that follows the river's twisting course to the lake. He crosses Kings' Bridge, arrives at Merchant Village. Bass tones carry between gaps in the streetscape. Past the storefront of a ski and snowboard shop, he sees shadows flickering on the sidewalk. A band is playing to packed tables in a former sewing shop. Nothing else is open on this Tuesday night. Going in, Tony regrets the creaseless collar and pleated pants he wore to work. The Shag, messy and eclectic, is the kind of low-budget dive Silicone played early on, tacky without irony. He orders a beer, watches a three-piece hip hop act play two songs, and leaves.

When Leanne comes home, they walk. A

space has opened between them. Their time together has a scheduled quality. The colours are leeched out. She wants to talk about it, just not at this time in her career.

A new agent is in the office across from Tony's, a suited up brunette with porcelain skin. She's worked in real estate before, but took an extended leave. Charlotte's filmic beauty unsettles Tony. She's put together in too many ways, the finishing school profile of a trophy wife. He suspects she has a fiercer side that has lied well and often.

The moniker 'divorcee' is the only evidence of her married life. He finds himself listening for the click of her door when she comes in. He's said nothing to her that he wouldn't tell any new agent at the brokerage. And nothing suggestive from her, no wandering eye to parse out for deeper meaning. When she's back from showings on her third day, Tony leans in her doorway. "How'd it go?"

"Y'know the place on Navy Street?"

"Can't miss that palace," Tony says. "Any takers?"

"A couple who want to live on the lake

said the kitchen's too small for entertaining. Give me a break. Pardon me, I haven't been off my feet all day." Charlotte crosses one leg over the other, takes off her shoe. "Wasn't sure I could do this job again." Tony watches her rub the arch of her foot. She pretends not to see him gawk. A smile tests the corners of her lips.

"Why'd you get out of real estate?" Tony says.

"Didn't need the money. I found hobbies. They kept me interested for a while. Then they weren't the right hobbies."

"How so?" he says.

"Let's say I need to be accountable." She packs up her desk and says goodnight and Tony feels robbed.

———————

Leanne isn't home when Tony comes back from the gym. He inspects their small garden for blanching and defects, looks over his shoulder when cars approach. He wanders along the street browsing gardens. A half hour later he's on an overpass to the original settlement. At the water's edge, the destination of his walks with Leanne, he thinks about the lines of Charlotte's outfit, and her skin underneath it.

Tony's asleep when Leanne gets home. He wakes up to the memory of Charlotte massaging her foot. He cancels viewings, won't leave the brokerage as long as Charlotte's there. He asks her to lunch. She says she has to make a call. In seconds she's at his door with her purse. "I'm set if you are."

The Main Street patios are packed with retail staff on break. High sun bakes the ground and a cool current blows in from the lake. He hasn't thought out his opening gambit, doesn't want to. There's no engagement or wedding band on Charlotte's hand, just an heirloom opal on her middle finger. He'd like to ask how her marriage failed, but that might draw attention to Leanne. "You picked a helluva time to return to real estate." Tony laughs.

"I'm in no hurry to earn commissions," Charlotte says.

"Glad to hear it. Paul's thought about leaving. Arthur can't cover the overheads."

"If I quit I'll waste away," Charlotte says. They talk around their living arrangements, skirting details, where and with whom. When plates are cleared, Tony orders another drink.

Charlotte asks for the bill.

They lunch together three times that week. He tries to prolong the meals, but each lasts as long as Charlotte takes to eat it. When she finally asks about Leanne, he doesn't downplay her impact on his adult life. Charlotte likes hearing what drew him to Leanne. She says less about her ex, won't discuss Don unless pushed, says that she'd rather Tony "drop it."

Her reluctance to answer basic questions about herself makes Tony think she's putting him off. She describes the house Don built by the lake. The self-described homebody doesn't match the profile he's pieced together of her. "So you tended a mean garden and did community work? That didn't bore you?"

"Who said I wasn't bored?" Charlotte says.

"You're not the type," Tony says.

"What type am I?"

"The type who lives in obscenely modern boutique hotels. The furniture is red and uncomfortable."

"You mean I'm cold?" Charlotte says.

"I mean you're not the tearoom type. You

belong at thousand dollar-a-plate, charity galas, charming philanthropists."

"Been there, done that. Good at it too. But I was role playing."

"Not like now?" Tony says.

Charlotte tells him about her last job. She worked as a masseuse in a massage parlour while Don was at work. Barring abuse, there were no restrictions on the services the masseuses provided, if they were consensual. She's told no one except her friend Sandrine and a former real estate client, Sam.

At first she ignored the occupational hazards. Excitement outweighed the risks, the novelty of the unknown client. Then came the sexual assault, or was it rape? It's why she quit, so that the pleasure of the job wouldn't eclipse the fact she'd been violated and inure her to that kind of treatment. Don had no idea.

Updating the listing of a late-day sale, Tony notices the light on in Charlotte's office. *Leanne said she'd be late*. After a day of solitude, poring over contracts and floor plans, he knocks on her door. "Dinner?"

"Maybe. I'm not that hungry. Let me guess, Leanne working late again?"

"Yup."

Charlotte slides contracts into file folders. "I think you're entitled to a dinner companion."

"Not out of pity?"

Charlotte takes off her reading glasses, looks up at him. "No, I really want to join you."

7

It's gusty and hot. Thunder cracks over the lake. Warm wind billows their clothes. Tony's tie whips his chin and he stuffs it in his shirt. Charlotte chooses the restaurant, a corner spot with a patio overlooking the river. He doesn't tell her that Leanne works across the river.

Tony insists that they eat inside. Leanne sometimes crosses the bridge for lunch. She's sat at this very table many times. He doesn't know what Leanne does in the hours she says she's at work. In fact, she's at work. When he thinks of avoiding her he misses her, wonders how her day has been.

The meal is terse and guilt-ridden. Not a word passes between them when he walks her to her car. Spending so much time together — both think but haven't said — is tantamount to cheating. Her Buick, a popular make at the brokerage, reminds him of a hearse. She wrings her mouth into a smile, opens the door to get in, then reverses course, slams it, steps onto the curb. "Why'd you ask me to dinner tonight?"

"Why'd you agree to come?" he says.

"You looked like I feel when I go home, desperate and alone."

"Why did you and Don split?"

"Is that important? I know you're attracted to me."

They walk south of Main Street to Lakeside Park Pier. Charlotte talks about her compulsive return to the parlour, her curiosity when new clients came in. "I'm in control most of the time, then I surprise myself." They start back down the pier.

"I'm not judging."

"And if I said I was raped?"

Tony's stops. "On the job? Did you go back to the parlour?"

"Yup."

He shakes his head. "I wouldn't have guessed. Still waters run deep, I suppose."

They watch the sunset across the bay on glass towers. Charlotte hugs her chest.

"Since we're being honest, here's one: I think a lot about straying from Leanne."

"Why haven't you?"

"I've tried. But I know where it leads. That doesn't mean I still don't think about it a lot."

"How long have you been together?"

"Three and a half years. Is fidelity so uncommon?" Tony says.

"I was true for eleven years. I find cheating is usually a matter of the right opportunity with the right person."

"I'm not married yet," Tony says.

They walk to her car in silence. He thinks of going back to the empty house. Charlotte's hair flaps against the lace band of her undershirt as it rides above the neckline of her blouse. He takes her hand, leads her down a gravel path that ends under the bridge to Leanne's workplace. "What are you doing?"

"Just this once? Please, I won't ask again."

"Where are we going?" He doesn't answer. It's not his attempt to seduce that rattles her, but his reason for making it. *It's because I told him about the parlour.* She also wants to follow him down the path and feel all of his desire.

When he positions her against the

bridge's concrete pier, Charlotte knows she wants more encounters like this, just not with him. Tony pulls out her shirt and slides his greedy hand into her dress. For a moment Charlotte looks like someone else, inexperienced and afraid, and his fervor subsides. She looks away and he feels like a molester. She sees his shame and reaches down to restart him.

There's nothing to say on the awkward march back to her car. She knows he won't leave Leanne.

They have five more trysts over two weeks. Each fails to recapture the thrill of that first time under the bridge. They steal away to forbidden places – a public washroom, Lakeside Park gazebo, the garden behind the brokerage. Risk of exposure elevates an experience that would otherwise fall short of expectation. When they climb out of the shadows, there's little to bind them outside of their common weakness. In a hotel they could settle into a more domestic arrangement. Tony won't have it. Since hearing about the parlour, he's decided that Charlotte's secret history was the source of her mystique. That secret has been revealed. Where she might enlighten him on home design – renovating the lakeside manse skilled her in the art of subcontracting — he has no interest. Her feminine wiles have nothing on Leanne, whose latest production is her best, the reinterpretation of a dated play that relates Napoleon's childhood loss of his father to postmodern humanity's sense of impermanence. Using history to allegorize the present is an old trick. Leanne's production challenges audiences. In Silicon her writing challenged Tony.

Hormones play by their own rules, and Charlotte's beauty still cuts through him. When he picks up her scent in the corridor of the brokerage, sees her legs on the way past her office, his resolve melts. If Leanne knew about Charlotte, she'd leave. They'd discussed the scenario. She's not the long-suffering wife who looks the other way.

Tony cuts short calls, files contracts, runs upstairs to invite Arthur to golf. The third floor has a balcony with a view to the lake. In better days, Arthur invited Tony outside for cognac and cigars, a chance to luxuriate in the continued success of Ashfield's number one selling realty. A couch has been parked in front of the walkout for weeks. Arthur takes advantage of the realty's reduced hours to work on his golf game. He keeps busy, listens to the petty ramblings of agents with too much time on their hands. His refusal to take a dim view of people is a trait shared by Tony's father, a trait that Tony wished he had. An adolescent surliness underlies Tony's interactions that he's been unable to outgrow.

With more to lose as franchisee than other agents at the brokerage, Arthur's the one least rattled by the housing crisis. Tony's resisted getting too close to him. If Tony strikes out on his own, they'll be rivals. Today he could use mentoring — and a distraction from Charlotte.

The first time that a client fired him, Tony was skipping meals as a new agent, running a retired couple to showings in Ashfield's North End. They'd expected their dream home to come cheap. He was also selling the house they'd called home for twenty-eight years. He couldn't unload it, but not for want of interest. His clients wouldn't budge on a price Tony warned them was too high. Rejecting all offers, they dropped Tony's services without notice, breaching their three-month contract. Arthur took Tony out on the balcony, offered him a cigar. "They've stolen enough of your time," he'd said. "Don't give them another second."

Arthur offered Tony the long view in these conversations, warning him about the cumulative effects of stress. "Forget what can't be fixed." Tony gained perspective and his new poise reassured clients. He'd lived the paradox behind the drums, trusting instinct instead of overthinking the pattern of beats. On a skateboard, he'd learned to relax into a launch and stay calm in the air.

Tony can't explain why clients turn sour on a home. He knows building code, can rewrite a lousy agreement in his client's favour. It's in negotiations that he stumbles. His dad, a retired accountant, could advise him on markets: home starts, building permits, inventories. It was his father's grasp of human nature that was lacking. Until the record deal, Tony didn't discuss the band with a man who'd played it safe his whole life. "Dad doesn't get music," Tony carped after rehearsal. Arthur wagered his net worth and beat a path back from bankruptcy to lead Ashfield's largest realty. He's Tony's idea of a success, a risk taker who's found a modicum of joy. Tony thinks highly of his dad, but there's gloom in the man's caution.

"Don't go home for your clubs," Arthur says. "I keep a second set in my trunk."

They climb out of the cart. Arthur addresses the ball.

"Did it get easier when you became a broker?" Tony says.

"I don't work less if that's what you mean. Clients don't roll through the door in this climate."

"Tell me you worked harder early on. You're out the door by three every day."

"It's not about hours."

"If the day comes that I have more time, is this how you suggest I pass it?"

"That depends on your drive." Arthur blasts a three hundred-plus yard shot down the middle of the fairway.

"I don't have the discipline for sport."

"You had it for music."

"Once."

"I worked up to this. I used to drink for any reason, to celebrate a sale or to lick my wounds through a slump. Then it was ladies. Flitting from one girl to the other. If one really wanted me, I thought there was something wrong with her, and was onto the next one. I couldn't reign it in. Almost lost Linda because of it. I have an addictive personality. To beat a bad habit, you need a healthy substitute. Golf's held my attention so far."

They walk through the next hole, buy drinks from a booze caddy. The course boundary is a fast-flowing river. Arthur and Tony stand on a footbridge where fly fishermen are flicking lines. "What was Charlotte like when she started?" Tony says.

"More heartbreaking than she is now. Too much woman for her age. She didn't know her hold on men. She knows now. Some of the older male agents tried to protect her. Me for one."

"Was she – I don't know – happy?"

"She was less jaded. She was young."

As Tony pulls out of the course lot, a woman in a Buick the same colour as Charlotte's pulls in. She's older than him and looks familiar. Youthful good looks are still evident in her smooth cheeks and round supple lips. He u-turns back into the parking lot, checks in front of the pro shop for her golf partner, parks, looks in the entrance window. Then he remembers: Arthur's wife Linda.

He calls the house to see if Leanne's back. No answer. If the woman wasn't Arthur's wife and he could've bedded her, he would've. Having nothing at home for dinner, he stops for groceries, walks the ready to serve aisle. It's a trick, putting store-bought food into pots to pass off as his handiwork. Leanne knows right away, finds the printed cous-cous and chow mein cartons in the recycling.

This time he buys an uncooked chicken, cashews, basil, cilantro. He breaks the spine on a cookbook, makes basil chicken, Leanne's favourite. It's late and he's famished, but he'll wait for her to come home and join him.

Leanne, smelling the lemony steam, leaves her bag at the door. "When did we last eat together?" she says.

"I can't remember." They share a bottle of Chianti and take an unsteady walk to the lake.

"Why'd you go all out?" Leanne asks.

"Arthur talked about finding healthy substitutes. I need to try."

He has no appointments the next day, no idea how to handle Charlotte when she comes in. Before, on the days she left the office before he did, she'd duck into his office to say goodnight.

Today he doesn't see her. Is she in her office, door closed to him as a form of punishment?

He grabs his gym bag, knocks on Charlotte's door. No answer. He opens it. She's in her chair reading a prospectus. "I can't keep this up," he says. She looks up, lowers her head, resumes reading. He leaves.

Tony can't sleep. Until Charlotte, his deceptions seemed minor. He hadn't considered himself a cheat. He calls the number Darren gave him that night at the Cameron.

"Didn't expect to hear from *you* so soon," Darren says.

"Didn't plan to call so soon. I had to know whether you miss the band?"

"I don't miss that last year after the tour. Getting sentimental, Tony?"

"Life was simpler then."

"Maybe. I run from band to band. None of the work is very stable. I love playing though, songs of addiction and women who leave you unsatisfied. Music's where my hunger goes to feed. Wouldn't mind more money though, a nicer pad."

"Money does buy that," Tony says. He

thinks about his old room on the landing, a gallery of rock memorabilia. The new house has none of him and Leanne, its walls bare save for Kandinsky and Klimpt prints from the AGO gift shop. They've decorated the way they think they're supposed to.

"I tour sometimes with Plunk. Pay's alright."

"I appreciate talking to you, Darren. Say 'hi' to Nathan." Tony digs through a box of old notebooks in his basement, takes one out with a glossy He-Man warrior on the cover, leafs through the poems and lyrics penned in a child's loopy scrawl. Together they represent an ample body of work. There are incomplete songs he'd planned to polish fifteen years ago. He lands on an unfinished verse:

When I think I'm standing still

Buried in a picture

He stares at the page, then the words come:

The past is gone; you're with me now.

The future's in your eyes.

He gets into a rhythm, writes two more verses. In Silicone a writing bout lightened his day. The mood in which he started a song, no matter how dark, fed the writing.

Tony sold his studio gear when they came to Ashfield. It doesn't matter. He doesn't want to record. It's playing that counts. He sets up half of his sixteen piece kit, climbs behind it, guitar slung over his shoulder, his notebook open-faced on the floor beside him.

Tony goes outside, stretches out on the deck, falls asleep. Leanne finds him there watching the stars. "Do my work hours upset you?" she says.

It's a trick question. He's expected to say "yes," but he's used to being alone, wouldn't know what to do with her around. "I miss you and I'm okay," Tony says. "You don't exist for my entertainment."

"Are you happy?" Leanne says.

"Not if you're miserable. Work all you need to." Leanne lays down beside him. They hold hands and watch the sky in silence.

Arthur's in the lobby. He can't sleep past seven, comes in early though there's no realty work. His kids live out of province. Linda works all hours. His fear of not knowing what he's missing has worsened with age. He likes greeting agents as they come in. The receptionist hasn't arrived yet. When Tony comes in, Arthur's in her chair.

"I meant to ask at the golf course," Tony says.

"Shoot."

"Are you honest with Linda?"

"Are you kidding? I'm as honest as she can handle."

"Is marriage a lie?"

"Marriage is role-play," Arthur says. He leans back, interlocks his hands behind his head. "It's an agreement about a script whose chief theme is tolerance. If marriage can't accommodate the life you want and think you can have, get out." He swivels his chair, checks the hall for eavesdroppers. "I've been faithful for a long time, but I won't let a weak moment ruin what we have."

"Don't secrets keep you apart?" Tony says.

"They can keep you together. I could've been less of a stranger to Linda. Maybe you're a better man than I."

———————

Tony and Charlotte treat each other like addicts in a recovery program, bonded by the resolution to stay apart. She updates him on her divorce proceedings, suggests places for him to daytrip with Leanne. When Charlotte returns to the office from late day viewings, his lusty pangs return, but he finds white collar distractions: coffee, administrivia, golf.

In the off season, Leanne plans a trip to New York to lure top billing shows to Ashfield. She and Tony stay in a brownstone hotel off Midtown Fifth Avenue and expense martinis in splashy Upper East Side restaurants. It's their first real trip since Silicone's cross-Canada tour. Tony feels hip again. Sitting on outdoor furniture at rush hour, he watches a chess match between an NYU student and a bag lady. A street artist is painting a circus on the sidewalk of 7th Avenue. Hundreds of office workers traverse the median, running the orange hand signal. "So what do you do?" the student says.

"I'm in sales," Tony says. The student, a scrawny twenty-something woman in braids, has nothing more to say to him. Tony feels remorse. Quitting the music scene cost him more than the band. He's out of step with the pace of contemporary life. He'd underestimated the advantage of momentum. If he'd stayed in the band, could he have kept pace? In New York he realizes that Leanne has kept up that pace. She moves in higher circles than he does.

To have more experiences like New York, Tony plots to make more money. Charlotte helps him secure rich clients. She knows what they like. Don insisted on the toys for their home: in-ground sprinkler system, movie-viewing room, under-floor heating.

Home prices bottom out, but the losses may be irreversible. Tony takes out a full-page ad, lists each home at seven figures. The commission on one sale is more than he earned in his entire first year as an agent. The old staging tricks won't cut it: fresh coat of paint, mirrors to create illusory space. Harvey Shnacter, an ex-marine from Montana who lives with his mother, commissions Tony to do the impossible: find the acrid woman a home of her own that she'll like. Tony subcontracts the renovations. All of his other work is pushed aside. He has to offload viewings to rookie agents.

The gap between his life and the one he'd pictured for himself, though the picture has never been clear, is bigger than he'd like. He's forgotten how to dress down. His social engagements are work-related activities he wouldn't choose to do without a push from colleagues: golf Saturdays with Arthur, hockey Wednesdays on the Ashfield Realty-sponsored team. He enjoys himself once he's on the park-like fairway or bright ice of the arena, but a show is still his idea of a good time: musicians on stage burning to connect with an audience.

He takes a bag of jeans and a t-shirt to work. A thought's been spoiling the plan of starting his own brokerage: He'll always be a salesman. What won't he compromise to close a deal? Pouring on the charm, the self-loathing starts.

Tony changes out of formalwear in his office, gets to The Shag in time for a band called Elevator's last set. They're packing up their gear. Tony approaches the drummer. "I don't mean to bug. Just wanted to tell you the band sounded great."

"Well thank ya."

"How'd you get into music?"

"I was always drumming – on cardboard boxes, trashcan lids, saucepans. One day my dad came home with Ludwig bongos. I don't remember starting to drum because I've never really stopped. I'm Will, by the way."

Tony finds Elevator's singer folding the microphone stand. She's petite and pale and reminds him of an old friend. "You're the singer with the velvet voice? You've got quite the range."

"Thanks so much! I'm Felicia." She curtsies.

"Tony. I just met Will. Are you from here?"

"I am, actually. Music's been a diversion for me." She pulls a scrapbook out of a box by the stage. "I made this to remember my brother Sean." She plays him two songs that she wrote after Sean died, opens the book to photos of the trip they took to Pukaska National Park. "We sang under starlight from the top of a granite cliff. Our voices echoed down the lake." She closes the book. "I'm scared to leave Ashfield. Sean used sing for us. We played here once a month." The whole band seems unsettled to Tony. He thinks of himself at that age. Always worried, though he had so few responsibilities. He feels like he's among friends here, doesn't have to sell himself. Elevator's music rings true to him, the unfiltered emotion of Felicia's singing. Her voice is a war on desperation.

The Shag has an open mike between bands. Singers with acoustic guitars play two-song sets. The performances are guileless and hippy-dippy, the sort Leanne played in college before Silicone. The headliner Midnight Echo is up. He's seen the name tacked onto Main Street message boards. They're playing "Truckin'" by The Band. Tony grabs a drink and sits on a stool to see past the crowd. They play a few folk chestnuts. When he grabs his coat to leave the band launches into Creedence Clearwater Revival's "Fortunate Son." Seats and tables are pushed aside and the crowd's on their feet. Tony's dancing too now. The band plays a totally unoriginal sounding original. He likes the tinny retro guitars.

His shirt is drenched, as though it was him playing, taking a breather between sets, drying his face with a hand towel. Leanne's still at the Centre. He drinks in the smell of hairspray, sweat, booze; the hum of idling instruments; the heat of close, nameless bodies, sensations he can't find outside music and can't live without.

———————

Leanne opens the door to a thundering staccato. She knows Tony plays on the nights she works late, but she imagines him covering the songs of his favourite bands, like a bored teen killing time in his bedroom. She hides at the top of the stairs. He switches to guitar, sings. The song's about their lives together in Ashfield. She thinks its theme is disappointment.

She comes downstairs to where he's holed up behind stacked boxes. He stops playing, topless and sweat-drenched. "Don't stop," she says. Leanne feels ridiculous in her nylon jacket. Her work clothes are itchy and smart. She wants them off. Tony's game face is gone, the one she's used to, always on the sell.

She unclips the barrette on her severe bun, sits next to him on an upturned milk crate. He plays her the songs he's been working on, heaves boxes aside to get to her guitar. She tunes the strings that uncoiled under a capo she forgot to remove. They huddle together playing counter melodies.

———————

Leanne came at Tony's urging. The Shag makes her giddy. She remembers sneaking into places like it underage to see bands. The bartender with the Karl Marx beard looks like her favourite professor. The walls are hung with concert announcements, album covers, vintage gum wrappers. Mannequins dangle in the glass storefront. The docent from the art gallery beside the Centre is at the bar. Leanne elbows her on the way past, says, "Watch this," and looks for a place to set up, an edge of carpet and two amps the only hint of stage.

They've been preparing for a month. Leanne could've waited to perform. Tony couldn't. She likes the freewheeling quality of diving in with a rough sketch. Her voice still has that sweet vulnerable quality that makes Tony ache. He climbs out of his kit to play guitar on the next song, launches drum samples on peddles. Guests stop talking. The crowd is small. She tilts her bass, adjusts the pickup volume. Leanne is hooked, but the two-song set is done. They could break the rules, play "Astrofix," Silicone's big hit, making them instantly recognizable. But Tony puts away his guitar. Leanne kisses her bass, says, "Let's do this again."

8

When Tony announces plans to leave the realty, Arthur takes the high road, promises to market 'Team Tony,' offers him the brokerage lawyers and accountant. Tony will lease the top floor of Arthur's manse, sign a non-competition agreement that limits client defections to the upstart upstairs.

Before planning the move, Tony waits in Charlotte's office for her to come in. "Can I talk to you?" he says.

"Everything alright?" Charlotte says.

"I'm starting my own brokerage. I'd like you to be a partner."

"A co-owner?"

"You don't have to buy in. I'll cover your portion of the lease for the first year."

"Thanks for thinking of me, but no way."

"Really? You have a solid client base.

Why not have total control, keep more of your money?"

"Be in charge of others when I'm barely in charge of myself?"

"Well there is that. You could say the same of me. I'm not so resolute or self-disciplined."

"You need autonomy. I couldn't go it alone."

"I'd be there too."

"The blind leading the blind?" Charlotte laughs." Tony smiles.

"Arthur's not a better agent than you are. He's just further down the road in life. I need to be around people who've already made most of their mistakes."

"You'd make a great broker though," Tony says.

"My goals aren't work-related."

"If you need anything, I'll only be upstairs."

Leanne wins an appointment to the Centre's board of directors. They don't invite her to golf, but her advice is held in high regard. She's head-hunted to program theatres across the North East. Her set work is cited in the Contemporary Theatre Review and the New York Times. It wouldn't be a stretch to quit the Centre and join a big house: Mirvish in Toronto, the Actor's Studio or Lincoln Centre in New York. The Board ups her salary to preempt a departure.

Leanne calls her dad to share the news. "You put in too many hours," he says. "Stress multiplies free radicals. You'll get cancer!"

"I won't quit the Centre." Leanne and her dad talk about the boats in Lakefield Harbour — the tall clipper, the sloops and small craft. They made wooden models of liners when she was a child. Nautical terms bring back the steady nestling and gluing of fragile parts into place on their living room table. It's the unsaid childhood idyll they cling to. "I'm in trouble at work," Leanne says.

"You just got promoted. You've designed how many sets?"

"It's much more than stage work. The board approved building an amphitheater on the river and expanded the summer schedule — on my recommendation."

"You'll be fine."

"It's too late to pull out. Shows are booked for an unbuilt venue. I'm expected to design sets following schematics I can't read. I told the Board that adding theatre space would make the Centre a regional powerhouse."

"You set yourself up."

"Thanks, you're a big help." He doesn't want to hear about her job. She remembers Dad's working life, each new project one more self-abnegating compromise with management. Work demoralized him. *How quickly Dad forgets.*

He passes the phone to Anne, Leanne's mom. "I wish you could see the doll house Emma built! I just bathed Ben and read to the kids," Mom says. Since Tina had kids, their exploits are the mainstay of these calls.

"It's not too late to have kids," Anne says.

"Please stop. Remember what Dad said on grad night? 'I wish you a life of your own choosing.'" Words had a finality that night. Friends saying goodbye before going to college.

"That's just something people say, Dad," she'd said in her prom dress at the passenger door. "You can't imagine a life for me different from Mom's."

Leanne thinks this phone call could be ten years ago, so little has Mom changed. "I think you do as you like," Anne says. "We just wanted you to have a sensible job and a supportive husband."

"I'm good at a job that I love. Tony sets no limits on my ambition."

"He hasn't married you yet."

"That's our decision." Leanne ends the call, finds Tony reading. "They're asking about kids again." He's glad it's them asking, wants to know her answer.

Tony doesn't think kids would be a sacrifice. He stocks carbon fiber hockey sticks, Calloway golf clubs, parabolic skis, all the toys he wants. His den is a mancave with a home theatre on the scale of a sports bar. He has surplus time and no plan to fill it.

Leanne meets Sandra and Victoria for coffee. They choose their college hangout: Simone's Tea Room. Neutral ground. The place is how she remembers it, a mix of college students and patients from the Centre for Addiction and Mental Health next door. The friends talk film and books. Their references are dated. Culturally all three of them are out of the loop.

The theme of Sandra and Vic's kids dominates the conversation. Feigning interest, Leanne asks questions about them that she doesn't care to have answered. Who of the friends, she thinks, has made the greater sacrifice? She feels guilty, like the kids she doesn't have — might never have — are on a street corner somewhere, waiting for her. She lies, tells Sandra and Vic she's meeting a roofer to discuss the re-shingling of her house, and drives back to the Centre.

Leanne's noticed that many of the women she meets on boards of directors are single. Some had been married or living common law. Was giving up their partners a choice or a job requirement? She ponders this, having given the night to a production for which others will get the credit. She doesn't know how Tony can tolerate her work schedule. He hasn't made her choose. He puts no pressure on her at all.

There's pressure enough at work. Knowing she'd contributed to a winning production used to be motivation enough to fuel her through the next one's launch. When *War Horse* ends, she dreads staging *The Caretaker*. Firing her Person Friday sent staff a message: Leanne does the important work. To delegate now would seem out of character. She has herself to blame for staff's reliance on her.

She leaves the Centre early. One more call to a supplier won't make a dent in preparations for The Caretaker. Tony's out. She practices the songs they've been working on, takes a walk. It's sunny and quiet. She comes to a park. A girl runs through the playground, trips, lands hands-first on the gravel. "Are you alright, sweety?" Leanne says.

"I'm okay." She chokes back tears. "You're my neighbor. You build stages." Leanne doesn't recognize her.

"I'm really a songwriter," Leanne says. The girl runs to her mom, who kisses the scrape. Leanne takes a second look to make sure the playground family are real.

Her neighbours, the park, the route she and Tony take on their walks, seem foreign. Why does she feel like an exile? She'd call it depression, but she's not sad or lethargic. She considers her roles in people's lives: her charges who are obliged to deal with her; Sandra and Victoria, who've gotten used to her absence; her parents who won't talk about her job. She misses Tony, who's learned to occupy himself without her. She sits on a bench in the empty playground. *If I disappeared, would I be missed?*

Tony's still not home. She calls Victoria. "Thanks for thinking of me," Vic says. "It's only been — what — four months? One call would've sufficed."

"I'm not the only one with a phone."

"You're the busy producer. I didn't want to disturb you," Vic says.

"You're the swamped mother."

"All the more reason to call. I need the pretense of a life. I wasn't always a mother."

"How's Sandra? When I call it's like entering a room where someone's just dissed me. I'd hoped she was over Tony."

"Sandra feels ripped off, like you have the life she should've had."

"She seems happy."

"The give-away is her silence. She was never stuck for words before Pete. He's an attentive husband with no aesthetic sense. That's hard for a designer. Sandra overestimated the upside of a man she wouldn't have to work at pleasing. Every schlocky sitcom he watches, every tacky shirt he wears, reminds her of her compromise. She won't bring him out, says he's uneasy around new people. She's the uneasy one. I watch her wince at his corny jokes. He's like an ADHD kid off his meds seeking constant stimulation. Sandra's distinctly unstimulated — part-babysitter, part-wife."

"She thinks that's what I have, mental and physical stimulation?" Leanne says.

"You don't?" Vic says.

After catching up on the kids' extra-curriculars and the latest stagings, they rehash their art school days. Leanne sits through anecdotes about Vic's husband like a torture to be endured. The phone call reminds her how different they've become. What happened to their big plans? She likes to think she's living the dream, that Vic and Sandra are the ones who've settled.

When Tony comes home, Leanne's huddled on the couch. He kneels down beside her. "Take a break. Live a little," he says. At his urging they've gone out with other couples, work friends mostly. The women distrust each other. Without fail, a caddy remark is dropped or false complements rain down. Leanne always comes away feeling evaluated. At the Centre she's heeded the warnings about 'fraternizing' with employees and trusts no one. Celine in lighting brings Leanne pastries. The gifts stop when Leanne doesn't promote her to a vacated senior position.

You think everyone has an angle," Tony says.

"I'm no one's fool. I hear you, finding fault in people is hard on the soul."

Leanne returns to the park, watches a mom rock her baby while her other kids, a boy and girl, crawl through plastic tubes. The younger of the two slides out of one of the tubes, runs to Mom. Playing grounders while Mom nurses on the bench, they trust that she watches out for them. Leanne remembers when she started to distrust her parents: sixth grade, lugging a Christmas gift she'd made at school. She'd soaked holly branches, shaped them into letters, which she glued above a sleigh dressed with felt. Thinking the gift destined for the mantelpiece, a treasured childhood artifact, she ran into the house to show her mom. Leanne bounced on the spot, waving the card. "You made that?" her mom said. "Nice."

In the morning, scraping the remains of breakfast into the garbage pail, Leanne saw the card smothered in last night's spaghetti dinner. She stopped showing her work to Mom.

Charlotte has time to kill before the next showing. She's snacked away her appetite. After a needless reordering of her desk and a chat with the receptionist, she takes a walk. The brokerage is vacant. The agents who'd straggled in late before lunch have gone to viewings. Charlotte walks down Main Street, its boulevards freshly primped by the Ashfield Horticultural Society: tulips and daffodils in half-barrel planters; light standards festooned with banners of pastel pink and turquoise. Main Street is pristine, an Alpine village landed on the north shore of Lake Ontario.

Town Council's attention to detail is borderline psychotic. The few narrow strips of parkland are mown to stubble, weakened at the roots by excessive watering. The Senior Citizen Green Team stalks stray garbage on the sidewalk. Charlotte doesn't get how the overpriced shops stay afloat and doesn't care: The town gives her a lift.

She enters a small bookstore, skims the bridal magazines, stories of bridezillas who'd ransom family for their Big Day. She'd done it too: two years of planning; fittings for shoes and dress; tours of garish venues; meetings with photographer, caterer, tailor. Her wedding was the peak of her marriage, the beginning of the end.

She hears the quiet crack of a torso arching over her shoulder, assumes the person behind her is reaching for a magazine that she's blocking. She steps aside, but the body steps into the space she's created, too close. She feels indignant about having to move yet again. Maybe the man is joking and knows her, that friend who covers your eyes from behind and says, 'Guess who?' She adjusts her stance to steal a glimpse. The man is of average build, the young end of middle-age, wearing a red shirt. He's grinning. She doesn't see his whole face, doesn't need to: the man who assaulted her at the massage parlour. Her legs feel pinned down. She wants to vomit. She's been expecting to bump into someone from the parlour. Did it have to be him?

She crosses her arms, looks once more at him full-on. Instead of withdrawing, he stares into her, smiling broadly. Charlotte mouths, "Excuse me," since no sound comes. She runs out of the store, handbag swinging.

She sprints down the sidewalk past the idlers and walkers ahead, scared that turning to see if he's there will trip her up. The visual field dissolves and she swoons, even as her legs gallop forward. One block from the brokerage her legs give out. Charlotte hunches over, coughs into her hand. Her breaths deepen and she's up and running again. She doesn't recognize landmarks. Coloured lights flicker, the frame-by-frame of a hand-operated reel to reel.

A hand grips her shoulder. She slips out of it, falls into a forward lunge. He's panting behind her. "Watch where you're going!" a playful voice chimes in from the sidelines, as though witness to a lovers' tiff.

He's arm's length when she reaches the brokerage. The receptionist is on the phone, scrolling through vacation properties on the desktop. Registering nothing or ignoring the clap of blinds against the glass door, she nods at Charlotte, who makes a beeline to her office. Charlotte doesn't mention the man waiting outside. He seems to know she won't tell.

Charlotte falls in her chair. When she thinks about faces at the parlour, it revives in detail, the candle-lit rooms and folded linens, the reception booth with its half-wall barrier. She peeks down the hall, sees the man through the glass door guarding the entrance, returns to her desk. She thinks through scenarios that include calling the police. In each one her secret history is made public. She won't call. Tony heard Charlotte come in and hovers in her doorway. She waves him off, lays her head on her desk, falls into a breathy sleep. Tony's back at her door when she awakes. "Pull out a cot why don't you? You snore like a drunk."

"I'm late for my appointment! Was I loud?" Charlotte fingers a spot of drool on her shirt.

"No one's here. I'm waiting for my favourite client, Sam," Tony says. She checks her compact mirror, locks her office door. But the man in the red shirt is still outside, glowering like a disgruntled worker waiting to rough up his boss. She pads to Tony's office, loses her footing, falls against the wall.

"Are you alright?" Tony says.

She's vertiginous, wants to vomit. "Remember why I left the parlour?"

"You got a scare. That man, the one who"

"—raped me?" She sits down on the edge of his desk.

Her account of the chase doesn't surprise

him. "And he's here now?"

"Check for yourself." Tony has cut down on exercise since getting back into drumming, but thousands of hours at the gym have left their mark. From reception, he sizes up the man outside. Tony's client is late. If Sam comes now, he might get hurt.

Tony tucks his shoulder, barrels through the door, sends the man outside skittering backwards. He grabs the man's shirt, "That's how you operate, haunting the ones you attack?" The man says nothing, push-kicks Tony, breaks his grip. Tony chases him between the brokerage and the building next door to a vacant, fenced-in lot. The man climbs the fence, snags his pants on the rubber-coated wire. Tony lifts him off by his waistband. The man catches hold of Tony's leg, topples him. They trade headshots. Tony rolls him onto his chest, cranks his arm up his back. "Sorry — I said I'm sorry!"

The man squirms out of his shirt and Tony's hold, except for the cuff, which he holds onto with both hands. He wins the shirt tug of war and runs. "Damn it," Tony says. He kicks the crushed stone. The man is gone.

Tony's client is waiting at the brokerage. Tony relisted the home Sam wanted but couldn't afford. He should've ditched Tony. Instead, Sam extended Tony's contract. "What happened to *you*?" Sam says.

"Late is all. I ran here. Sorry." Sweat beads down his face and neck.

"Everyone on the run. I just saw a colleague from school running in dress pants."

"Hold up," Tony says. "Your friend was running in dress pants? Was he wearing a red polo?"

"Yeah, just saw him on the way here."

"Your friend's in real trouble."

"Yeah, that's Clyde."

There's a home in an Old Ashfield cul-de-sac with ribbon windows and a herringbone chimney. It's Arts and Crafts and no style in particular. When it came on the market eight months ago, Tony drove past it with the ambivalent mix of admiration and antipathy that characterized his attitude toward Ashfield. One Saturday in August he requests a viewing. His firm purchase offer is accepted the same day.

In the fall Tony and Leanne book a resort

package in Shanghai and upgrade their car leases. Leanne oversteps at her sister's that Christmas, arriving in her Jag wearing a Tracy Reese wrap dress. Tina answers the door in the frumpy housecoat she wore in her teens. "Another car, already?" she says. "I get it, you have money." Leanne wilts. Established Ashfield society pay Tony and Leanne no heed. Nouveau riche like them couldn't buy their way to an audience. Leanne trades in the Jag for a Civic and lets her wardrobe slide. It doesn't change relations with Tina. In rags Leanne would outshine her.

Leanne writes out invitations for the christening. Tina and her mom will be pleased to attend a Catholic baptism. Six months ago Leanne and Tony began attending the small church by the lake, a track record that Father deemed sufficiently Catholic to marry them and baptize their son.

Leanne's mom commandeers the front pew for extended family. Tony's uncle whispers to Leanne, "Your mom's in her element."

"Yeah well, it's her show. I'm glad she's happy." She looks down the aisle at her sister. Tina's in a loud black and white dress, clinging to her purse. Leanne considers her own stiff onesie and coiffured ringlets. The sisters have never looked more alike.

Charlotte watches from the back row. Leanne recognizes Tony's colleague — *she's more of a work friend really* — *or just a friend*. They met at a brokerage Christmas party. Arthur had reserved a hotel balcony at the height of the housing slump, a venue Leanne had thought excessive for the times. The mood was one of forced joviality amid murmurs the realty wouldn't see another Christmas. Arthur's rousing thanks for years of service came off like a retirement speech. Leanne remembers Tony's face. She'd seen it the night his dad died, the rudderless look of a man who'd lost a role model.

Across from Leanne, a dark-haired woman dabbed her cheek with a napkin. Her eyes tracked Tony as though they guarded a secret that only he shared. Leanne took Charlotte's stare as a reaction to something Arthur had said in his toast:

> *The downturns remind us that a house's value isn't its curb appeal, location, or grandeur. Home is where we can be ourselves among friends. The brokerage has been my home these last twenty-eight*

years...

Leanne thought the dark-haired woman was upset by the last rites Arthur had given the brokerage. It wasn't the realty's purported imminent demise that troubled Charlotte, but the hold that Tony still had on her. She was over him. Then he stood up to the man who'd raped her.

Charlotte hadn't seen Clyde since the chase. She'd altered her drives to and from work, jogging down the back roads, secure in her knowledge of the lanes and private drives. Then came the calls, first Tony's then Sam's, identifying the man in custody. Clyde was a math teacher whose conduct had drawn suspicion at the board office. After the rape conviction that secured his dismissal, more accounts came forward: colleagues alleging sexual harassment, sex workers alleging sexual assault.

Clyde's high-risk antics had escalated in the lead-up to the arrest. He'd already been suspended from teaching and had found work as a tutor. Besides assault, he was charged with possession of a controlled substance. Police didn't elaborate on the nature of the evidence to media. School board and police shared an understanding of how far this man had fallen, the withered regard that staff and students still held for him.

When Charlotte's testimony recounted the night at the parlour, Arthur and Paul reserved judgment. Even her ex-husband Don fit the parlour into the bigger picture of the space that had grown between them. Charlotte is still haunted by Clyde. He leers from a blind at the periphery of her dreams.

Tony hoists a squeaking Jacob over the baptismal font. Leanne thinks Charlotte looks happier than when they first met.

A churchy, bright brass band of pink cherubic men with wispy beards is playing out of sinc. Leanne taps Tony's arm — a signal from Silicone days — to see if he caught the players' mishap.

Silicone still gets radio play, mostly on retro nights, mostly late. At the church reception hall, Tony puts on their CD. He used to get embarrassed hearing it in public. He'd poke fun, call their sound "derivative." Serving cake while the second track "Carbon" plays on the hall's tinny sound system, he's impressed how well it holds up. The tension of the band's last days seems quaint, like a childhood aversion to onions.

"We weren't very unique," Leanne says, "but we were hot."

Tony says, "Our lyrics take you somewhere. The sound is catchy and timeless. What more could we ask of our music?"

"To make us rich?" Leanne says.

"More money would've kept you in the band?"

"A lot more money."

"Would you leave the Centre for any sum?"

"I didn't used to think so. I'd walk away for nothing now, if I had somewhere to go."

Tony builds a drum kit from broken stands, a tom-tom, snare, and symbols he's collected since he started drumming. He reclaims the stands with a blowtorch and copper pipe. Leanne says, "Don't get ahead of yourself. Jacob might not take to music."

Tony says, "He could go further in music than we did."

"And saddle him with our unfulfilled ambitions?"

"That's what parents do, pass down their dreams."

Charlotte's beauty hasn't spared her from the estrangement of single life: playing third wheel at couples' parties; the predatory, cougar sexuality men ascribe to her. She declines invites from old friends to get-together, sick of being perceived as a threat and pressured to explain her singleness. She withdraws from the singles scene, where the self-interest of both genders is on full display: the crass desire of men and the trickery of women hunting for providers. She's free again tonight. When the brokerage empties and the phones stop ringing, the quiet is piercing.

She eats at a bistro, takes a walk, crosses streets to avoid the hungry calls of men leaving bars. Outside the drop-in centre where refugees and exiles gather during the day, Charlotte remembers her grandfather's advice: "Service is the best form of healing. Helping others takes the focus off of yourself."

She returns here in the morning. The drop-ins are refugees from inside artificially-drawn, colonial frontiers in Central Asia and sub-Saharan Africa. Melinda, the volunteer coordinator, runs the program out of a former dance studio. She answers the door in a yellow taffeta dress, gives Charlotte a tour. Melinda's a self-taught artist and single mom. A retired personal support worker prepares snacks in the kitchen while new intakes fill out profile cards. Charlotte's job is to read the cards, assess skills and interests, and start each intake on a career search that might never end.

The walls are decorated with Melinda's paintings: rural scenes of barns and abandoned farm implements, maritime scenes of tall cliffs and rough seas. Each work has a price tag attached. Her donations provide a revenue stream for the program. "You're self-taught?" Charlotte says. "Why haven't you left Merchant Street? You must've made a killing from painting."

"If people like me keep leaving, the village won't change."

Twice a week Charlotte jostles past the line at the door, guessing the origins of dialects. Today's intakes are from Sierra Leone, former child soldiers with blood on their hands. She helps them write resumes. More counsellor than job agent, she listens to their stories of abduction and drug-induced coercion to kill. She tells them not to give up, thinks she's better at giving advice than taking it.

Tony climbs three flights to his office, roots through the resumes of the inexperienced agents he hired. He summons the new hires to the foyer before opening. "Don't worry much about marketing. Selling's about relationships," he says.

"I put full page ads in both Ashfield papers," Craig says.

Tony likes Craig's suit and wants to deflate him. "Ads can win you an introduction. After that it's about trust."

"I thought it was about selling?" Craig says. Tony regrets hiring him. During interviews Craig's confidence was a refresh from the smarminess of the other candidates. It may be a liability. "You'll burn through new clients if they think you haven't worked and won them the best price," Tony says. Sean checks his watch. Marissa reads a text. Tony remembers ignoring Arthur's warnings, thinking he knew better. When sales fall through, they'll seek the voice of experience, Tony's voice.

There are three women on his team. Rita has a young family and no spare time. She's broker material and won't stay with him long.

Madison is overwrought. Her hair and makeup look like hard work. She marks entries in a pocket calendar, though there's no work to schedule. Odette is a distraction. She has an artless quality that Tony feels bound to protect and an unaffected beauty that he lusts for. He's restrained himself from making advances. Where he thought parenting would kill his attraction to Leanne, it has restored her to him. The discipline she brought to the band, keeping Nathan and Darren in line without bruising their fragile egos, has nothing on her parenting skills. Leanne's defense of Jacob is fierce. Tony's grateful she's the mother of his child. He thinks she's more giving than he is — and more careful.

Tony likes playing brokerage overseer, filling in when agents can't make it to viewings, negotiating messy, complex sales.

Leanne drops by the brokerage with Jacob before her maternity leave runs out. They picnic in the back garden. Raising Jacob is a come-uppance. Tony feels a strain of rebellion in his son that will give meaning to the humiliation of aging. This is as much control as he'll get as a parent. The rest of fatherhood will be a steady letting go.

Leanne lets grooming slide, buys fewer clothes. Her narrow eyes give her away. Last night's leftovers petrify on the kitchen counter. Laundry billows out of the bedroom doorway. Tony feels it too, rocking Jacob while Leanne catches up on sleep. They're shattered, yet he can't conceive of life without them.

Jacob flails in the vinyl papoose strapped to Tony's chest. Leanne packs the remains of lunch. They walk to Lakeside Park, pass benches with memorial plaques sponsored by the families of honoured dead. Tony lays Jacob on the grass and sits on a bench beside Leanne. The benefactors might've chosen this spot for the view. Maybe it was a treasured picnic spot or the deceased moored a boat here. The park is on the former homestead of one of Ashfield's founding families. Leanne imagines a woman watching from the belvedere for the steamer returning her husband from war, a boy watching for Dad to resurface from the boat launch in the town's shipbuilding days. From this vantage point facing the river basin, Ashfield looks as it did two centuries ago. He likes the bench with its plaque and epigram. What would his plaque say if he joined the ranks of dead memorialized by park benches?

Leanne watches a young man in a dory row out of view. The light on the pier rotates in its housing, an outline of moon against the sunlit sky. Tony walks Jacob and Leanne to her car. Rather than returning to work, he walks to the Sunrise Diner. The priest from St. Paul's, Father Adrian, is talking to someone at the back. If Adrian hadn't made eye contact, Tony would've taken a seat facing the other direction. He thinks he got roped into having Jacob baptized. "Religion's a delusion," he told Leanne, "enslavement by fear to blind faith." Tony comes to their table, shakes the priest's hand. Adrian says, "You remember Father John? He retired."

"Father John, of course. Do you miss St. Paul's?"

The three talk hockey and weather. Father Adrian excuses himself, "I have Reconciliation soon. God bless you and your family, Tony." John stays at the table, leans back, stretches out. He doesn't look old. If he didn't know better, Tony wouldn't peg this man as a priest. Adrian is always on message, a priest by all appearances. In Tony's estimate, John's views are born of experience. His faith has been tested and he's barely passed. Tony gets a sense of who John was before he became a priest. If religion couldn't erase the man behind the collar, Tony figures, there must be something enduring about him.

"How's Jacob doing?" John says.

"He's a happy boy," Tony says. "I worry about his future. You've seen a lot of changes, Father. Are young people different today?"

"When I was ordained in the Seventies, people expected to work for things – cars, vacations, leisure. Somewhere along the way we lost patience."

"People still want to work, Father. Life's expensive. Unemployment is high, maybe permanently so. A lot of young people are doing without."

"Austerity's not so bad. It can help you find joy in simple things – friendship, nature."

"I've never got the priest thing," Tony says. John smiles, signals the waitress for a refill. "All that solitude and celibacy." Tony's suddenly aware of the old leather jacket he's wearing normally reserved for nights out. He feels defiant.

John says, "It's not all sacrifice. There are selfish reasons to be a priest."

"Your job takes a certain kind of person,"

Tony says.

"The world takes all kinds of people. A life well lived isn't easy."

"But why dumb it down with angels and demons?"

"To make sense of the whole shifting, hostile mass. When you find your place in the order of things, the world's a friendlier place."

"Religion's an illusion. People need hope I guess," Tony says.

"Don't underestimate the power of living by a vision."

"I hope we can continue the conversation," Tony says.

Before John can respond, Tony gulps his coffee and reaches for the retired priest's hand. An abrupt close, but John doesn't balk, "I enjoyed our talk, Tony. Hope you have an umbrella. It's dark out already."

"I'll be fine." Tony tucks his chair under the table. The priest grabs his arm. "Keep it simple, Tony."

"I don't know what you mean."

"Appreciate what you have."

"No, Leanne's the ambitious one."

"Don't get lost."

"I have to go," Tony says. He heads for the brokerage. The sky is hung with thick bands of cloud. He feels a few light drops, but it's warm and he wants fresh air. He cuts down a parallel street, skirts the brokerage, crosses the bridge to the edge of the original settlement. The sidewalk ends. He's on the shoulder of a busy arterial road when the downpour starts. He'll miss an appointment if he doesn't head back. Tony's running now. He turns around at the red brick lakefront home he sold yesterday. It's unrecognizable. What's changed? Thirsty and soaked, he stops at a variety store to buy water. Rush hour traffic crawls east. A long row of vehicles rolls forward and grinds brakes. He lopes back across the bridge and through the ageless comings and goings of the original settlement.

Made in the USA
Charleston, SC
16 December 2015